POINTED ARROW

WINGS OF ARTEMIS 12

REBECCA ROYCE

Pointed Arrow (Wings of Artemis 12)

Copyright @ 2020 by Rebecca Royce

Ebook ISBN: 9781951349400

Print ISBN: 978-1-951349-48-6

Cover art by Syneca Featherstone, Original Syn Covers

Content Editing: Heather Long

Copy Editing: Jennifer Jones of Bookends Editing

Final Proof Editing: Helayna Trask of Polished Perfection

Formatting: Ripley Proserpina

Published by Rebecca Royce / RARE Publishing, LLC

www.rebeccaroyce.com

Dearest Reader,

Well, we are here. The very last book in the Wings of Artemis series. This is an incredibly bittersweet moment for me. This is the twelfth novel I've written in this series since 2016. There are also two novellas in this series, so a total of fourteen stories I got to tell. Wow. This is the longest series I've ever written, and it was a privilege to get to tell each and every one.

What started with an idea about a woman who had no memory and was "kidnapped" by her husbands (plural) moved to the story of her daughter and what happened to her. And then suddenly she had a best friend who was miserable living on the other side of the universe. Once her story was told, I needed to tell you all about her sister-in-law who was having an absolutely terrible time at the hand of her father. Oh, and then that once miserable friend had a sister too. She had been living a lie on Earth for long years, and she needed a story. Somewhere in there, I told a small story about a woman who woke up on a pirate ship, and she had her story to tell. Melissa. Diana. Paloma. Waverly. Amber. Priscilla.

And finally, that brought me to Sienna. The thing about Sienna is she was the first female heroine I wrote in this series who wasn't connected at all to the other women. Amber rescued her, but she was in cryogenic sleep when that happened. She isn't someone that anyone really knows. She is an outsider. So, I believe, are her guys. She is from the Dark Planets, the completely misunderstood part of the universe that most of our other heroes and heroines have never been to before. Or not for very long.

That's okay. The outsiders are going to save everyone. And when that is over, they won't be outsiders anymore.

With love and gratitude for every word you read or listened to,

Rebecca Royce

This book is dedicated to YOU. With all my thanks!

ACKNOWLEDGMENTS

Well, things never get written in a bubble, and certainly a twelve novel, two novella series did not. So let's see who I need to thank for all of this. This is a huge list so please don't be upset, I'm just going to use first names. Ripley, Chandra, Heather, Jennifer, Becky, Meghan, Helayna, Jax, Cara, C.L., Lane, Autumn, Julia, Syneca, Lia, Ralph, Austin, Sawyer, Duncan, Gene, George, Joss, J.J., The Doctor, Mom, Dad, Kathy, & You (Most of All, Scarecrow.)

WHO IS WHO IN THE WINGS OF
ARTEMIS

Who is Who in the Artemis World:

Just in case you got lost in the twelve books and two novellas.

Our heroines and heroes:

Kidnapped By Her Husbands/Rescued By Their Wife —**Melissa Alexander.** Love interests: Cooper, Nolan, Wes, Dane, C.J., and Geoff. Daughter Diana, son Asher, and other younger children.

Crashing Into Destiny/Reclaiming Their Love—**Diana Mallory** (daughter of Melissa Alexander & Geoff Mallory, introduced in *Kidnapped By Her Husbands*). Love interests: Damian, Sterling, Cash, Lewis, & Judge.

Meeting Them/Loving Them/Saving Them—**Paloma Delacroix** (best friend of Diana Mallory, mentioned in *Crashing Into Destiny*). Love interests: Tommy, Clay, Keith, and Quinn Sandler.

Ship Called Malice—**Priscilla**. Love interests: River (introduced in *Loving Them*), Bo, Jordan.

Dark Demise/Light Unfolding—**Waverly Sandler** (half-sister of the Sandler brothers on their father's side, introduced in *Saving Them*). Love interests: Ari (cousin of the Sandler brothers on their mother's side, introduced in *Meeting Them*), Jackson (introduced in *Rescued By Their Wife*, and seen again in *Reclaiming Their Love*), Canyon (introduced in *Crashing Into Destiny* and again in *Reclaiming their Love* and *Saving Them*), Rohan (introduced in *Reclaiming Their Love* and again in *Saving Them*).

Still Waters/Rising Tides—**Amber Delacroix** (introduced in *Loving Them* and again in *Light Unfolding*). Love interests: Amari, Hunter & Shane Chen (introduced in *Loving Them* and again in *Light Unfolding*).

Lost Star/Pointed Arrow—**Sienna MacKinnon** (introduced in *Still Waters* and *Rising Tides*). Love interests: Trenton (introduced in *Loving Them* and again in *Light Unfolding* and *Rising Tides*), Wade (introduced in *Light Unfolding, Still Waters,* and *Rising Tides*), Blaze (introduced in *Light Unfolding*), Anders (introduced in *Light Unfolding*), Corbin (introduced in *Light Unfolding*), Kellan (introduced in *Light Unfolding*) and Devil (introduced in *Rising Tides*).

The Bad Guys:

Sandler Cartel (destroyed)

Garrison Sandler (deceased)

Evander Corporation (from the other side of the galaxy, bent on world domination for the purpose of commerce, constant changing leaders, creator of Super Soldiers.)

THE SMALL SHIP we were in jolted in the air, and I held on for dear life, wishing I could be back on the hot, rainy, miserable planet we'd just escaped. Trenton, who was flying the small vessel, didn't notice my discomfort, nor should he since he was, in fact, saving our lives. His concentration belonged elsewhere. But Wade, who sat strapped in next to me, sure did.

He leaned forward, taking my hand in his. "Whoever designed and built this thing was obviously not concerned with the dampeners. It sucks." He side-eyed me. "I might even puke."

I highly doubted that. Wade and Trenton were battle scarred, and I doubted that space travel would make either one of them blink an eye in worry. But he was sweet to say that to make me feel better.

I didn't miss the way his gaze traveled to the number on my wrist, telling him just how alive the infection inside of me currently was. It hadn't changed. I was still at a level seven, and that was higher than any of us wanted it to be.

"I think it's more likely they were repaired badly."

Trenton rolled his eyes. "We're not spending a minute more on this thing than we have to. As soon as I can get parts to repair her, I'm going back for the ship."

I cared about Artemis. Somehow, in the few days I'd been conscious on her, I'd really come to feel fond of the old lady. But I cared about who we had just left there a lot more. Without people on it, a ship was really just a ship. Wasn't it? What did I know? I'd only been consciously aware of being in space for a matter of about a week. Or maybe less. Time was becoming something I lost track of regularly. It changed from planet to planet, ship to ship, space station to space station. In any case, it didn't matter.

I was missing five people who should have been here with us.

Blaze, he led everyone with so little thought to himself. Anders, he was sweet inside and a caretaker despite that not being his role in life. Kellan, he didn't see how he was kind because he was trained to see that as a fault. Corbin, he knew how to fix everything and wanted to be there for everyone. And finally Devil, he had not started out with them but came to join us because he wanted to be with me, because he wanted redemption for the life he'd lived before he'd started over. He was smart and kind, even if he didn't know it.

All of them were somewhere else, not with us. Raising my free hand, I bit down on my thumbnail. "I'm asking again, how can we just leave them?"

"Because Blaze told us to." Trenton didn't look up. "And the general agreement all seven of us have is that we are putting you above everything else. I assure you, I won't rest until we have them back from wherever they are. If they're hiding down there, then let's assume there is really a good reason for it. If they've been captured or killed, then we have to run. But we're not abandoning them. We're just regrouping once we have you safe."

I was so sick of being the reason they were constantly at risk, and I was even more annoyed at having absolutely nothing to contribute except as someone they could make love to or make out with when it was safe. Not that I hadn't really enjoyed that. I absolutely had. But it couldn't be my only role. That was pathetic.

Clearing their emotional pain wasn't particularly useful right now, and I had no one to zap.

I let go of Wade's hand, smiling at him, and turned back to Trenton as I swung the chair around to face the controls. "What can I do?"

"Do?" Trenton shot me a quick look I couldn't decipher. "You want to help fly?"

"Yes. What if the two of you were suddenly rendered unconscious? How would I fly? Can I help make it less bumpy?"

Wade leaned back in his chair. "You're nicer than me. I'm not offering to help."

"I noticed." Trenton laughed. "Okay, Sienna. You want to fly? I'd love the help. Put your hands on the two buttons like I am. They're not push buttons; you have to rotate them. Do you understand?"

I actually did. I held on to it. Funny, I could feel the ship differently when I touched the controls. As though it moved through my hands while my body continued to bounce in the rough turbulence.

"I'm not going to let you fly right this second. Too much instability until we exit the atmosphere and head into space. Then I'm going to haul ass to Mars Station. But hold on to the controls with me so you can feel what I do. You should get the sensation of what I'm doing as I'm doing it. This is a teaching trick on vessels like this one. Artemis is different. But we'll start with this."

Wade rose, holding on to his chair but seeming really unconcerned with what was happening, which only added to my already solid belief that he really wasn't as freaked out as I had been from the bouncing.

"I'm going to go check out the medical supply situation here. I left most of our stuff on Artemis locked up in a fridge. I didn't want to risk losing all of it. Hope that wasn't a huge mistake."

That meant that he was concerned about me and the looming seven on my wrist. I was worried about it, too, but less so every day than I had been on day one with it. At this point, the last thing I needed to worry about was the viral number and my complete inability to control it.

Wade abruptly stopped, lifting up his tablet. "I've got contact."

"Who is it?" Trenton still didn't turn to look.

Wade scrolled his fingers over the screen. "It's Kellan."

"Is he okay? Where is he?" The ship jerked as Trenton pulled us clear, the turbulence fading as we broke orbit. He still hadn't taken his eyes off of the control panel. I swung around to fully regard Wade, releasing the controls. I'd get back to it. I wanted to see Wade's face. He was better at hiding things with his voice than his facial expressions.

He chewed on his lower lip. Not a good sign. "They're taken. He got a message out before they grabbed their devices. Says to dump the tablets."

Trenton swung around, letting go of the controls. "Take mine. Put them out the airlock. Evander took all of them. How did that happen? Our guys are better."

I loved that he was so confident about them. It filled me with warmth for a second before cold took me over.

Evander had them? Didn't that mean they would soon be dead? "Trade me." I spoke the words fast. "Give me to them."

"No," they both answered quickly, and I wanted to throw something. Why was it so constantly the case that everyone else could risk themselves for me and not the other way around?

"You know what? I have some fucking self-determination." Yep, I'd cursed. "Maybe if I say that I want to go trade myself for people that I have—in a short period of time—grown to deeply care about, then that is exactly what I want to do."

Wade shook his head. "Sorry, Sienna. I know this goes back to when we didn't listen to what you wanted. But we are listening. We hear you, and we're saying no because we deeply care about *you*. Maybe even more than you do about us, because we've all been fighting to keep you alive and safe for a long time. Before you were really conscious to know that." A muscle pulsed in his jaw. "We'd all die to do that. Don't lessen their feelings or their sacrifice by insisting on invalidating what we've done by throwing yourself in front of the exact people who want you. What they would do with you would be so much worse for the galaxy. Do you understand?"

I did because they kept repeating that over and over. I knew they were right. I wasn't an idiot, but neither could I stomach the idea of losing those I cared about in my stead.

Wade nodded at me as he exited with the tablets, presumably to put them out the airlock. I placed my head in my hands. Okay, I had to think.

"Trenton, I understand we can't give me over." I started with that as I lifted my head.

He smirked at me. "Trying to pacify my response?"

"Yes." Why bother lying? "But hear me out. Could you tell them that if they hurt the guys, then I won't give myself up? But I will if they agree not to. And then obviously we're lying and I don't." I shook my leg. The ship was steady now, but all I wanted to do was to shake some more, apparently.

He sighed. "We don't communicate with Evander. We beat the shit out of them, or we escape them."

"Okay, yes. That's what you've been doing. But this is different. There's one giant ship out there. Looming. Stalking. Fighting. It's the last one, and yet it seems to be getting stronger, not weaker. Any minute, it might figure out how to break through the black hole and bring reinforcements. But for this second, they're here and they're alone. If you could find them, you would bring in a big armada right now and take them down. Do I have that all right?"

He cleared his throat before he leaned forward and took my hands in his. "You do. You have that all correct."

Trenton's hands were rough, like he'd done a lot of work with them over the years. That was so sexy. I leaned forward before I rose and climbed on his lap. If he thought we were in danger, he'd have been paying me no attention right now. It must be an okay moment. "Then maybe it is time to do something differently. What do you think?"

He smirked at me. It shouldn't have been so adorable, but it was. "Are you pressing yourself against me to get me to do what you want?"

My heart raced. "That's not the only reason."

He threw his head back, laughing. "Sienna, when I get you alone, when Wade isn't about to walk back in here, and when I'm not responsible for a craft that shouldn't be flying in space anymore, I will gladly give you whatever you want as I get you naked. Trust me, I am walking around in a perpetual state of hard wanting you. But for now, I have to keep my head in order and not think with my dick. Thank you for trying though. You on my lap is the best thing to happen to me today."

"Trenton." I ran my hands over the scruff on his cheeks. "Thanks for keeping me alive last night."

We'd been lost in the rain, and he'd found us shelter. I didn't want to imagine what would have happened to me without him.

He nodded. "I'd die to keep you safe."

That was quite a statement. "Okay. But please don't."

He cupped my cheek. "I'll do my very best." He kissed my chin. "Do me a favor and let Wade look at you. I need to know that you're as set as we can make you right now. Then we'll strategize about where we are running in order to regroup. My vote is Mars Station, but I know that's not your favorite..."

I shook my head, interrupting him. "Whatever works. I don't care where or how we do that. I'm somewhat steadier than I was when I was distressed there. It feels like a lot of time has passed and a lot of things have happened."

The second I said it, the more I realized I meant it. Yes, I didn't care where I was now. I just wanted Blaze, Kellan, Anders, Corbin, and Devil back. I wanted us all safe. Even if we had to spend the rest of our life in false orbit, with fake light, and no solid ground beneath our feet. I didn't care if the whole universe was shaky. I just wanted us together.

Climbing off Trenton's lap, I was bereft from missing his body heat. I shivered, rubbing my arms. It wasn't cold in here, so I wasn't sure what that was about. Trenton didn't miss that it happened to me. He leaned on his hand and spoke to me with raised eyebrows. "Go see Wade. Now, please."

I appreciated the *please*, but I had no doubt he'd pick

me up and carry me over to Wade if that were what he thought I should do right now. As it was, I agreed. The shuddering couldn't have been a good sign. With the ship mostly steady, I headed to the back where Wade stood staring at a small box of supplies.

"Well, if anyone needs to be rehydrated, the good news is I can do that with no trouble." He held up a syringe.

I smiled. "Think that would help me?"

"Well, it couldn't hurt." He held out his hand, and I took it. With his other hand, he stroked his fingers around the dials and readings that told him just how sick I was right now. "How do you feel?"

I took a deep breath. "Tired. But I'm not sure if that is because I really haven't had a good night's sleep in a while. I just had an incident of shuddering. Like I got the chills, but I didn't feel cold."

He nodded as though that made sense to him. "Anything else?"

"I think that's it."

Wade met my gaze and held it. "We're going to get you through this. I have some basic antiviral with me. It won't be as great as what I had on Artemis, but it can help right now. What I want you to do is come get some rest. Good old-fashioned sleep goes a long way, and when you get up, I'll check your numbers, and we'll see. If we're heading for Mars Station, you should have plenty of hours to get some rest. That bed doesn't look comfortable but will have to do."

He nodded toward the edge of the room, and I followed his gaze. He was right. It was a bed, but it looked more like a table. "I don't think this ship was designed for much of a long ride. We might be pushing our luck trying to get to Mars Station."

"Trenton can make a ship do anything he wants it to

do." Wade smiled. "Now if only I was this talented when it came to the human body. I'm limited."

Wade. I said his name in my mind because I knew that he'd hear it. He smiled at me. As it was our special thing we did with one another, I knew he'd understand how I felt about him when I did it. His gaze was heated when he met my own full on. "What has happened with me is not your fault."

"I know." He visibly swallowed. *But sometimes it feels like it is.*

The ship shook violently, and then a gush of hot air filled the room. Wade threw himself on top of me, taking us both to the deck.

"What is happening?" I yelled over my ringing ears. My head hurt. I might have hit it as we slammed into the ground.

"I don't know," Wade yelled back. Part of his shirt was singed and torn. Had he been burned? I didn't get to ask him because he was on his feet and rushing from the room. "Stay here."

Trenton. He'd gone after him. I got to my knees. Stay here? Not if they were both going to need me. I pulled myself to a standing position for a second before I puked. I couldn't stop. The need was overwhelming. That couldn't be a good sign. But that was the thing about vomit: it was all consuming when the need happened.

Wade dragged Trenton back in. He wasn't conscious. I lifted my head. "Is he okay?"

Shaking his head, Wade hauled Trenton onto the med machine in the far corner of the room. "No, but he will be. And you're obviously concussed. I can't do anything about that at the moment. Sit down. But don't lie down." He pushed buttons on the machine but didn't close it before he ran for the cabinet, pulling out a device. My vision was somewhat blurred, but I could see what it was.

"Isn't that Dev's device?" He'd used it in the station to hide our heartbeats from the others. He grabbed it and put it on Trenton's wrist before he turned to me.

With a nod, he closed the med machine. "Yes."

That told me nothing. I put my throbbing head in my hands. "Wade, what is happening?"

"We're going to be boarded any second, and I don't want them finding Trenton. They won't know he's here if they can't hear or sense him." He pushed the machine into the corner. "Have a silent mode. Have a silent mode. Thank fuck." It was like he spoke to himself.

"Wade?"

He rushed over to me. "Evander has us. They're tugging us on board their ship. It looks like they've managed to construct a super ship. We thought we had all of them. It's quite bad. My guess is that Trenton tried a maneuver that should have worked to get away from this mess, but it blew up instead because this ship sucks. They're going to tow us on board. Listen, this is important, and I have three seconds before I risk them hearing us. Trenton is not on here. Do you understand?"

I did. "I get it."

"Great. Whatever they do, survive." He kissed me, hard. I'd just been puking. It should have been gross, but it was one of the sweetest kisses of my life. "I love you. Just keep living."

Our burning ship jerked left, and Wade winced. "We're on their cube."

My head was thick, but I had to know how he knew this. "Has this happened to you before?"

"When they took me prisoner years ago to impersonate

me on The Farm. This is what they did. What comes next will be very unpleasant. But they need you, want you. My guess is they will fix your head. I don't know after that."

A loud bang sounded, and a second later the cabin filled with a spray. It stunk like something sour, and Wade covered my mouth and nose with his hand before he followed with a towel. "They're putting out the fire. It's a substance that stinks but isn't toxic. I'm unfortunately used to it."

I was having a hard time following everything he said. I closed my eyes, and Wade shook me. "No, stay awake. Easier to keep you healthy if you are. Aha, they're here. Evander Super Soldiers. Three of them. They're headed right toward us."

I should be scared, but the need to throw up rode me again, and it was everything I could do to breathe through my nose and try not to give into the need.

Wade rose to his full height. "Leave her alone."

"Move, doctor. Or I'll make this even more unpleasant for you. Where is the other one? The pilot? I was told there would be three of you. We're bringing you and the girl to the Vice President and getting rid of him."

I lifted my head. No wonder Wade had wanted to hide Trenton. He understood how these assholes worked.

"He died," I managed to say. "On the planet. He didn't make it onto the ship with us. That's why you were able to catch us."

"Well, that makes things even easier."

The three Super Soldiers were huge, but I was used to it from my guys. These three were completely clean-shaven. Short black hair, big angry eyes. My guys had really altered their appearances when they'd given up the hell that these guys lived with.

"Why do you even bother with this?" I rubbed my forehead. It didn't help the ache. "Evander is on the other side of the galaxy. Why not just let this shit go?"

Yep, I was cursing all the time now.

"Evander is our journey, our task, our home." The one closest to me bent over so his face was very close to mine. "And those traitors that you like might have forgotten that, but we never will."

"Hey." Wade leaped at him. One of the men behind the one currently snarling at me, intercepted and knocked him down to the ground.

My world spun. Then blackness.

THE AIR CONDITIONING on the Evander ship was high. Maybe I just noticed it so much as I slowly woke up because we'd been so hot on the planet. The small ship we'd attempted to escape on had been pretty warm, too. I shivered and rubbed my arms.

The movement must have caught someone's attention, because I heard footsteps, and then the awareness of a presence staring down at me from above proved impossible to ignore. I opened my eyes and stared at a stranger.

He tilted his head and smiled at me. "You're awake."

It seemed I was. But I didn't know who this was, and since we were on an Evander ship, I wasn't sure that I wanted to be. "Apparently."

"If you hurt her, I'll rip out your eyeballs." That was Wade's voice booming in the room. I lifted my head, careful to not get close to the man staring down at me as I looked for Wade. Some glass separated him from me. As he paced back and forth on the other side of that clear partition where he observed me, worry tightened the hardness of his jaw.

"Your doctor friend likes to make threats he can't possibly achieve." The man near me sighed. "If I didn't think we needed him, I'd put him out an airlock right now. I still might. It would be prudent for him to tone down his attitude."

I forced myself to swallow so I could think. "Who are you?"

"My name is Dr. Patrick Blume. I am a Vice President of Evander Corporation and in charge of this ship. I was charged with getting a hold of you, Ms. MacKinnon, and grabbing you, I finally did. I also managed to recapture some turncoat traitors to the company, and so I imagine management will be very pleased with me when we get back through the black hole."

They weren't getting through that hole. It had been officially closed down. That much I'd gathered from conversations I'd heard while I was on Mars Station. Did these people not know that? Or did they have some way to bust through the closed hole that we just didn't know yet?

As I didn't answer him, he kept speaking. Or maybe he'd have just done that anyway. Some people liked to hear the sound of their own voices more than they required any kind of response.

"Now the trick will be to keep you alive. And I feel I have the perfect solution. Your doctor over there, he found a way to keep you kicking." He picked up my arm. "I'm going to let him keep doing so because I believe I have the exact way to motivate you here."

I stared at him while I considered the best way to respond. Maybe Kellan was rubbing off on me. I just wanted to beat him to death. But instead, I swung my legs over the side of the medical bed that was more like a table. "If you think for one second that I—"

He held up his hand. "I know you can zap me. We've seen what you can do. It was impressive. You took down a Super Soldier when we tried to get you. I must say that was incredibly surprising. No, listen first. We have your doctor here. We have a spaceship full of Super Soldiers who work for me. And we have your men here, our former Super Soldiers, locked away where I can just as easily end their lives as I can keep them safe. All of that will depend on you and how much you are willing to cooperate with me during our journey."

Goose bumps broke out on my skin. I knew they had Wade. He was obviously stuck, or he'd be in here with me. But I couldn't just take his word that he had everyone else. He might have already killed them. I had to understand exactly what I was dealing with before I spoke anymore to this so-called doctor who was threatening me to comply with him.

And I had to somehow gauge whether or not they'd found Trenton, who we'd tried to hide on the small shuttle. What had happened with him?

But I said nothing. Keeping my mouth shut when I wanted to talk was something I'd learned how to do early on. I'd say very little and try to get more information than I gave.

"I need to see them. I'm not agreeing to anything until I see for myself that they are okay."

He lifted his eyebrows. "They said you were bright."

Who had said that? Who did they know that could possibly have told them that? My uncle who had initially sold me out to them? Did he know me well enough to make a statement like that? I didn't ask for clarification. That would wait. The doctor put his hand on my arm. "Easy. You were concussed. We fixed you, but take it slow."

I took a long breath. "Are you sure you should be in here with me? I might infect you with the diseases you gave to me."

He narrowed his gaze. "I was under the impression that Wade had gotten you to where you weren't contagious."

"Well, it's a day-by-day thing. You never do know." His statement had told me what I needed to know. Wade hadn't given him instruction on how to read the device on my arm. I looked down, and it still read a seven. Much as I wished it had magically gone down to zero, it didn't surprise me. If stress played a role in this, then I'd had my fair share.

This doctor, Evander's so-called vice president, didn't know that it had been at seven for a bit and that I wasn't a problem for him until it was ten. I wasn't going to tell him.

He scowled at me. "I think if you were contagious, then Wade would be dressed to protect himself from you. Since he wasn't, we're going to proceed that way."

I shrugged. "That's entirely up to you. You made me sick. You'd know best, I suppose. Show me my men. And then we'll discuss how things are going to go."

I might zap him if I could figure out how to get us all free. I could zap the whole damned ship if I needed to. Even if it knocked me out for weeks, I'd do it.

He walked ahead of me, which would have been stupid if a man hadn't come out of the shadows of the room to box me in from behind. He was huge, an obvious Super Soldier. But when I turned to look at him, I saw none of the light that I was used to in my guys' gazes. No, this man had dead eyes. I rubbed my arms at the goose bumps breaking out on them. Had my men been like this? Lost to nothingness?

Or was he just hiding deep emotion? I didn't intend to find out. I had a plan, or the beginning of one, and I wasn't going to blow it right out of the gate. Wade banged on the

|

glass between us, and I nodded to him, hoping he'd understand that meant I was okay.

He visibly exhaled a breath. There were dark circles under his eyes. How much had he suffered until I woke up? I wouldn't forget that he'd been through hell. Whatever happened next, I would find out finally how to make things okay for Wade. For all of us. Somehow.

What was funny was I was absolutely a prisoner right now. And yet for some reason, I'd never been so sure that I was powerful, that I was capable of doing what I thought I could do. This wasn't how my story was going to end. I was sure of it, and for the first time in my life, I believed in myself. Why the miraculous change had suddenly come on an Evander ship, I couldn't say, but there it was.

Wade banged on the glass, and I stopped to regard him again. "Let me the fuck out of here." He spoke to the doctor but glared at the dead-eyed Super Soldier who followed behind me. "Now."

I turned toward my captors. "I'd like him out."

"We can talk about what Wade will and won't get to have happen when we get back in here. If you don't want him left alone in there endlessly, then I suggest you hurry up."

It would be so easy to knee the doctor in the dick. It really would, and it was everything I could do to stop myself from giving in to the urge. Wham. He'd be rolling on the ground. Instead, I looked at the man following behind me.

"Why do you guys follow him? You're bigger and stronger than he is. What is he giving you to get you to continue with this charade? Your people are on the other side of the galaxy, and you're never getting back. Why bother with this? Find your backbone or something."

The doctor yanked on my arm. "Now, that is just what

I'm talking about. Your mouth. That isn't going to earn you any points speaking to him like that. They aren't going to turn on me. Or Evander. These men understand where and how their futures are laid out. They will be rewarded for their loyalty, whereas your men will be punished. That is the way of the universe. And if you think that black hole is closed, you underestimate our capability."

That was information I needed, and he'd easily provided it. Mental note, this asshole was easy to manipulate. I nodded at him, and he strode forward while I followed. We walked for a while, and I made notes in my head about where we turned and how many people I saw.

I counted ten other Super Soldiers, including the lethal yet silent man behind me, There were probably more. This ship was huge. How many people did it take to run it? I chewed on my lip when the doctor finally stopped.

He turned to sneer at me before he opened the door to the room. What struck me first as he gestured like he was showing me a new piece of art he'd designed was the blandness of the place. There was no floating air, no drift of sound other than a constant low-pitched buzz to my ears. Still, it was the scariest place I'd ever stepped into. "This, my dear, is where we keep people who we have placed in cryogenic sleep."

I sucked in a long breath. If there were ten, or more, Super Soldiers awake on this ship, there were hundreds upon hundreds of them asleep in pods in this room. It was a bigger space than all of Artemis combined. I rubbed my arms. All of that temporary confidence fled. Did every Evander ship have this many people on it? How had we not known it was this tremendous? Had the guys been fighting this all along or something else smaller and not understood this was still out there?

"It's impressive." He sneered at me again. "Xavier, show the woman where her friends are."

I loved how he downgraded what they were to me when he knew full well they were more than my friends. And by loved, I was, of course, being sarcastic in my own head. I hated it. With a passion. But I kept my facial expressions benign as I followed after the now named Super Soldier. Pod after pod was filled with people sound asleep, kept in a stasis until they were needed. People who fought for Evander. People who were very much what my guys used to be.

This had been their lives. Wake up, fight, maybe nearly die, and go back into the pod. Until one day, they didn't anymore. They had different experiences leaving this, each one of them in their unique way, but they'd done it. And now here they were, locked up again, and it was all because of me.

Right here was just what I didn't want, what I'd told everyone I couldn't have happen. I didn't want anyone dying for me. Or in this case, being put in cryogenic sleep when they'd had to endure this for so many years. All of this was because they'd tried to spare me this fate that I had now anyway.

My father should have left me to Evander to begin with. Then the beautiful souls who'd tangled their fate up with my own would not be in this predicament.

The sounds of the room hit my consciousness all at once. Maybe I was in some kind of shock, because I hadn't noticed how noisy the room was right away. But it was. There was a constant buzzing in the air. All of those pods made quite a racket altogether. Super Soldiers guarded the entrances and exits as though the people in the pods might suddenly wake up and try to flee. None of them made eye contact with me, and I couldn't help but understand why my guys sometimes questioned their humanity. There was something almost inhuman about the way these men seemed to stare through me, as though they didn't see me as *someone*. As though I didn't quite exist to them.

Xavier stopped, but I didn't need him to direct me where to look. To my left, lined in a row, were my guys. Tears flooded my eyes, and somehow, from an inner strength I didn't know I possessed, I managed to blink them away without anyone seeing them. Not that I could really hide it when Super Soldiers surrounded me. They could hear my heartbeat; they'd know the second that I sucked in my breath what I'd managed to do. Hell, maybe they could smell it.

I stared at my guys and forced all other thoughts from my mind. They didn't help, and I couldn't control what others were capable of doing or not doing. I could zap with just a thought. We all had our blessings and burdens. It was what it was.

There they were. Corbin was first and closest to me. His long hair was tucked behind his ears. I studied the dials and indicators on the outside. I wasn't sure what they meant. Heck, I couldn't even use the light switches in my bedroom before he'd showed me how. But I hoped whatever they said, it meant that he was okay. His face was the most passive I'd ever seen it, and I couldn't tell a thing by looking at him. *Please be okay*.

All of the men lined up looked the same as though the process that put them in cryogenic sleep caused that expression on their faces. I touched the glass.

"He's fine," the doctor snapped at me as though I'd asked him. I absolutely hadn't, so I ignored his remark. "But he doesn't have to stay that way."

And there was the threat. I'd known it would be

coming. I ignored that too. Next up was Devil. I'd never seen him when he didn't look somehow both tense and amused at the same time. But not now. It was as though he wasn't there at all. I took my hand from Corbin's glass and touched Devil's. I was going to make contact with each of them this way if I had anything to do about it.

Maybe they knew I was there. I'd reached out in my cryogenic sleep to Wade. It was possible.

In fact, maybe there was something I could do.

I pushed my thought at Corbin. *Corbin*. It was what I did with Wade. I hadn't tried it with the others. It had just been my thing with my sweet doctor. But now would be a really great time for it to work.

I wasn't sure if it did. He didn't open his eyes or reply in any way, but it seemed to me that the lights on his machine flashed quite a lot when I did that. Maybe that was some kind of response. I tried again. This time with Devil. *Dev*.

Next up was Kellan. His head was actually turned to the side with the same serene expression that I hated on the others. It was just unnatural. These weren't men who were passive. They were in constant struggle, even if it was in their own minds. *Kellan*. The sweet man who wanted me to zap him. He'd actually asked for it before he'd given me his utter devotion. I hadn't known exactly how to handle that, having never had it before. I was still trying to figure that out, and now more than ever, I was determined to see to it that we'd figure it out together.

Like the others, his lights brightened in intensity. Was it possible his even more so than the other two? I wasn't sure. I wished I could understand them.

If I ever got the chance to safely do it, I was going to ask Wade to explain it to me. Of course, that would mean deafening the Super Soldiers. Sometimes their extrasensory abilities could be troubling and not helpful.

Although more times than not, I was grateful for them.

I stepped toward Blaze, and my chest tightened. I was trying really hard to be brave about this, but there he was, the sweet man who led them all. He needed someone to look after him, but with that serene expression, it wasn't going to happen right now. *Blaze.* The same response greeted me. At least it was something, even if I was looking for something that wasn't there.

And finally, there was Anders, who had cared how I felt immediately upon meeting me. He was so kind inside I wondered how he didn't see it. I placed my hand over the glass and held on like it was the only thing that could keep me alive. Somehow, it felt that way. *Anders.* The lights lit up as the others had.

"You must really be some kind of a fuck for them to have all fought the way they did to try to prevent this from happening."

I stiffened my back. If Wade had been here, he'd have tried to hit him for saying that. I turned toward him. He wanted a reaction from me, a big one, or he wouldn't have said such a thing. I glanced to my left. Xavier and the others in here would certainly stop me if I attempted violence. Not to mention, he could probably end my guys' lives if I even reacted at all. He'd use my response as a means to hurt them. One button pressed and they might be dead.

"I must be." I smiled at him as though he'd given me a great compliment. As if I didn't want to rip his eyes out every second I was with him. "Shall we go back to the med bay? I'm afraid I need to lie down. I'm so sick." I pretended to cough, and he jolted. Yes, he really was worried about how sick he'd made me. Evander had a cure for me. They never made a disease they couldn't cure. Wade had told me that. But that didn't mean that this asshole in front of me had access to those cures. If he got sick, he might be as bad off as I was, minus Wade's good care to keep him going.

I needed to keep that in mind. I'd never wanted to hurt anyone.

He extended his hand. "You're not easily rattled."

"Why would I be rattled?" I stepped past him toward the door. Yes, let him think I was stupid, too. I'd never had to trade in deception in my life. My whole existence revolved around opening myself up and telling people the truth. But here I was, lying to this man, and I intended to do so until I got what I wanted—and that was all of us safe and out of here. "You made a promise, and I believe you'll keep it. If I behave, they'll be fine."

He blinked, and I watched as his expression changed in a second. Yes, he had just discovered I was a fucking idiot. Or at least that was what I was going to let him think from here on out.

I smiled. And I'd be a sweetheart, too. Well, I'd pretend to be. "Thank you for showing me the guys."

"You're welcome."

Yes, he thought he'd stumbled upon gold with me. I swallowed the bile rising in my throat and followed where he led. It had occurred to me, as I pretended, just how I was going to have to beat this man and take over the ship. The question was could I do it without killing myself in the process.

I stared behind me for a second as my guys vanished from view. I wouldn't let anything happen to them. Not ever. Even if that meant I had to feel the emotion of every person on this ship until they were so drained they couldn't keep their heads upright after.

I chewed on my bottom lip. This would be the biggest undertaking I'd ever attempted, and it would be absolutely fantastic if I could get my number down from seven before I did it. Although I might not have any choice. I couldn't control what my numbers did. If I had to take them down while I was at a seven or even higher, I would do so. I would point the arrow that was my strange abilities and weaponize them until I had back everyone I'd fallen for. They were mine. In the whole empty, cold universe, they belonged to me.

We entered the medical bay, and Wade stared at me through the glass. I could see the concern in the lines that appeared around his eyes. He was scared.

Wade.

I sent him the same feelings I'd sent the other guys, only he was awake to receive what I'd done.

He jolted, but only I noticed. Xavier remained in the room where he'd helped imprison my guys and had not followed us here. Maybe I wasn't deemed a threat. That was good. Let them think I was nothing at all. I preferred it that way. It wasn't the fact that I could zap them that would make me dangerous. It was the skills I used to help people that I'd turn on all of them tomorrow morning. Regardless of what my numbers said, that was what I'd do.

"Tell me, why does Evander want me?" I smiled at the doctor who had done this to me and who I would make sure couldn't hurt anyone I loved. "And how did you bring down my guys?"

The doctor poured himself some water but didn't offer me any. That was fine. I wasn't thirsty, and starting tomorrow, I'd have all the water I wanted.

"We developed a weapon that they couldn't resist. It disrupts the neurological functions of anyone we aim it at.

They are physically unable to move for hours. Your guys held up pretty well, even for Super Soldiers. I've never seen people who resisted so long." He winked at me. "And as for you, pretty lady, we want you to teach us how you do what you do. Disrupt the neurological impulses of people like a living weapon. You do that, and I'll see to it that you're not sick anymore."

Liar. He didn't have that capability. They'd have to bring me through the black hole to do that. "Sounds good, Doctor. But I'm starving, and I'm going to need some food before I can do that. Is that okay, please?"

He nodded fast. "Of course."

This man was so easy. Even a beginner manipulator like me could handle him. Easily.

3 / WHO TURNED OUT THE LIGHTS?

WADE and I hadn't uttered a word to each other in almost twelve hours. My plan to rest and recoup hadn't worked. I was too tense. I wasn't going to sleep when there was so much danger to the people I cared about. Plus, there were beeping machines everywhere. I couldn't even tell what they were hooked up to. The doctor had gone into his office and shut the door, but I had no idea if I was being watched. Or listened to. Someone was probably monitoring my heart rate from across the ship.

I rolled over on the table I was using as a bed and stared at the man I wanted to touch more than anything but couldn't reach. Wade wasn't sleeping either. He met my gaze in the well-lit room, another factor in my not sleeping, and smiled at me. There was no mirth in his expression. It was the kind of smile he might give someone if he were about to offer up the kind of news that would cause them pain. Maybe that their loved one wasn't going to make it.

I wasn't going to let that happen to us. Only good news from here on in.

Wade. It was all I could do, the closest thing I could muster to touching him.

He placed his hand over his heart, and it was as though he'd stroked my hand. I loved that we could connect that way, but it wasn't enough. I rolled over again. This really, really sucked. I'd take the shed in the rain over this. And thinking that just made me worry even more about Trenton. Was he still in the med machine? I had no way of knowing. Even trying to find out would place him in danger.

A boom sounded in the room right before the lights went out and then came back up a second later with the sound of a zap.

I looked around. What the heck had happened? Was that normal for this ship? I was on my feet at the same time Wade was. A quick glance told me that he had no more idea what had surged—I was pretty sure that was the word—the lights than anyone else. He was locked in the glass enclosure where I was pretty sure I'd end up in if I became contagious. But I wasn't. I strode toward the doctor's office just as he came out of it.

I had to be stupid, and I had to remember to behave that way. Somehow. "The lights flashed." I made the sound of my voice rise at the end so it wasn't clear if I was stating that as fact or asking it as question. Maybe that would make me seem confused, which I was, but not as much as I played at being.

"Yes, and I don't know why. Wait here. If you move, we will know," he threatened me as he strode out the door.

I waited until he'd exited before I ran over to Wade. I couldn't get in the glass room or talk to him since there was no way to get privacy with the Super Soldiers. There was too much to say to try to do it silently in our own heads. Small sentences and words, yes. Long phrases and tons of conversation, no. Still, it was nice to be close. There was such a thing as comfort just by proximity. He placed his hand opposite mine against the glass. I couldn't feel him, but I'd pretend I could. I was good at deluding myself, always had been.

The lights dimmed again, this time with a popping noise that followed. Wade dropped his hand and chewed on his lower lip for a second before he spoke. "Okay. The first time, it could have been some kind of surge, but no way this ship that almost caught us so many times over and over isn't well maintained. They'd have it fixed by now if it were something small. That means something has gone wrong. I'm not a ship engineer. I don't know what makes them tick, I just know how to point and go. But this much I know..." He let out a long breath. "That shouldn't be happening."

I digested what he told me. This was safe to talk about. Neither of us talked about the things that we couldn't say. Frustration had never been more palpable. To be so close and yet so far away from anything real.

"Are we in danger? I mean, not the obvious danger. I mean from the ship."

He shook his head. "No idea, really. Would be sort of ironic to survive all the things we've made it through and to die because of some kind of mechanical failure on an Evander ship, wouldn't it?"

The idea must have amused him, because he grinned. My tolerance for gallows' humor must have been low, because it was everything I could do to not holler at him to stop smiling in that moment. There was nothing funny right now, not even on the dark spectrum of things.

Several loud pops sounded in the room, and the ship tilted before it righted itself. "It's like it's dancing or drunk."

I spoke the words and then heard how ridiculous they

sounded. The doctor wouldn't have to question if I were dumb. If he heard me right now, he'd know for sure. How was I supposed to live up to my strange confidence that I could save us all if I couldn't even articulate things in some kind of verbose way?

"Dancing?" Wade caught my attention, and I waited for him to laugh again, but he didn't. Instead, it was like he thought about what I'd said in some way that made sense to him. I was glad for that since it didn't to me, not in the least. And I'd been the one to say it.

I sighed. "I guess it's just the way it's moving, it reminded me of a dance. It shakes a little bit, it turns a little bit. That's not a great description, but..."

"It is, actually." This time he laughed. "In the best possible way. Yes, the ship is dancing. That's exactly what it's doing."

Had Wade lost his mind? I'd assumed he was fine since they weren't giving him any medical attention, but perhaps I'd been wrong. "Are you okay?"

"Never better."

What? "Wade..."

He tapped on the glass. "Trust me."

I did even though it made no sense. Maybe some time, he'd get to tell me why it was so funny and wonderful that the ship was dancing. The ship tilted and then righted again before it did it again. And then again. My stomach turned. I didn't know how much more of this I was going to be able to take without vomiting. These were Super Soldiers who had bested us. Couldn't they get control of their own ship? This wasn't like Trenton when he'd been piloting the too small, not-ready-for-space shuttle that we'd tried to escape in.

The thought jarred me. *Trenton.* I bet he'd know how to make a ship shake. Was it possible? We'd left him unconscious on the shuttle. Was it possible he was here? Had they brought the ship onto theirs?

I turned to Wade. This time I sent him a different name to hear. *Trenton.*

Only he could hear it, and I couldn't communicate very much that way. When I'd been in cryo, I could do more, but awake, I didn't know how I did this at all. I just could, like breathing.

He nodded once. "Yep. Entirely that."

No one listening would know what we were saying. We'd done nothing to indicate what we meant if they were watching. There was just this moment that only the two of us would understand. Was it possible we were deluding ourselves? That we were totally imagining that this was Trenton because we wanted it to be him?

"What happened to Artemis?" I hoped it was okay that I asked this.

"They towed it in from the planet. When we get into the black hole, they're going to strip it for pieces. I heard them discussing it while they all got their vitamin shots or whatever they're being given." Wade sat down on the floor. "Go strap yourself in, just in case."

That was a good idea. I didn't want to get hurt, but then again, I had to be ready to take my turn to take out the doctor and others if the opportunity arose. If it was Trenton making the ship shake, that was great, and even if it wasn't, then I was still going to jump on this while everyone's attention was elsewhere.

"Wade." I still had something to say, and I didn't care who heard it. "I love you."

His eyes adored me, or at least his gaze made me feel like I was the only woman in the universe. "I love you, too."

Whatever else had gone wrong in my life, I would never

forget that for this time, I'd been the most loved person that ever lived.

I walked back to the table and watched the door. Was I just going to sit here and wait? Wade wanted me to strap in, but I couldn't bring myself to do that. This might be a moment for action. Did that make sense? I had no idea. For all of my gumption, I'd never done anything like this before. I'd never even really lied except to make someone feel better about, say, a bad meal or an honest mistake before all of this took place. By nature, I was an honest person, and my years acting like a spiritual advisor to others and taking away pain had made me more truthful, not less.

Although, perhaps it wasn't wrong to argue that I'd been a bit of a fraud in my role to begin with. It wasn't as though I'd ever really felt like I knew what I was doing.

"Do you think everyone feels like a fraud?" I asked Wade, aware it was random and probably out of place, considering where we were and what could be happening out there.

He stretched out his legs. "Yes. Sometimes."

He didn't even blink at my question, and that was just another reason I adored Wade. He rolled with things.

"Good." I walked toward the door. If it wasn't just me, then perhaps there was the smallest chance that I might get through this without getting us all killed. I heard him suck in his breath, but Wade didn't say another word. That was good. He could very well have given me away, and then I'd be done before I even got started.

What I had to hope was that in those moments, I was the least of anyone's problems. I was breaking the doctor's rules. He could hurt or kill everyone because I was doing this. That meant I couldn't fail.

I rounded the corner following the path by memory for the cryo chamber. Yes, the woman who couldn't turn on the lights was going to figure out how to turn off the devices keeping her guys asleep. I'd wake them. That was a good place to start, and then I'd take down everyone I could in the process. With no idea what I was doing, I entered the bland room that housed my guys.

I didn't want to hurt anyone accidently. No, I was going to be quite methodical in my dishing out pain. I rounded the corner and abruptly stopped. There should be a guard, at least there had been earlier, and it took me a moment to realize why he was missing. On the other end of the room, about to face off with two Super Soldiers was Trenton.

For the briefest of seconds, I was filled with joy before that turned into utter horror. He was never going to get past those Super Soldiers. They weren't ones I'd seen before, and I only knew Xavier's name anyway. Okay, I'd add two, and probably a ton more, to the count I'd made earlier.

Fine. I stared at the two about to launch themselves at Trenton, and I zapped the heck out of them. The energy buzzed in my head and took them both down. I didn't know that I'd ever given such force to my zapping before, but it worked. Both Super Soldiers were down for the count. I had no idea for how long, but we'd have to make do for however long that was.

I was saving my real power for a larger group of them. It wouldn't do to start out in small numbers.

"Trenton," I shouted, but he was already running toward me. We met in the middle, right by Anders's pod.

"You're okay!" He tugged me toward him. "That was quite a distance you blasted."

I hadn't thought about it. "I'm okay. So glad you are."

He'd been in bad shape when last I'd seen him, and he was still wearing Dev's device that gave him some ability to hide from the Super Soldiers. "We need to catch up, but while those guards are out cold, we need to wake the others."

Trenton whirled around to stare at where I indicated. "I wondered where the fuck they were. How about Wade?" He was already moving away from me to count the pods in the room and spot all of our guys.

"Locked in a glass box in medical. I left him there. He's not going to be happy."

Trenton made a sound in the back of his throat that I was pretty sure was a noise of agreement. Yes, he thought Wade was going to be pissed, too.

My engineering-oriented love started pushing buttons on each pod. "This will wake them. We're going to keep the rest of the Super Soldiers in here out cold. Let other people deal with them. I'm only going to concern myself with our people for now."

The door opened, and ten Super Soldiers ran in, followed by Dr. Patrick Blume, the idiot I hoped I never had to see again when this was over. Maybe he could just dissolve into space.

But I didn't want to hurt Trenton. "Get in the pod with Blaze."

"What?" He swung around, seeing the rush of Super Soldiers as he did, because he grabbed my arm like he was going to pull me away from them. I yanked my arm back.

"Just do it, Trenton. Trust me. Now."

I didn't wait to see if he'd listened to me. I had no time for that. Usually this was the kind of thing that I'd brace for, but I just had to do this, I had to take on the emotional pain of everyone on this ship until they were all sucked so dry they couldn't stay upright. I fisted my hands. Truthfully, I didn't know if I could even brace myself. I'd never attempted anything like this, ever.

I was going to take down Wade, and I had no idea if Trenton getting in with Blaze would work. It was possible all the sleeping Super Soldiers were going to get hit as well.

This was just the best I could do, the only hope we had.

I opened myself up, letting down my guards until I was fully opened to take on the pain of anyone who breathed the same air as me.

I closed my eyes.

The rush that hit me was beyond that of anything I could ever have imagined. So many people and so much distress. I'd known that the Super Soldiers lived in hell. Certainly, I'd experienced Anders's version of it when I'd done this with him.

But really... I'd had no idea.

Locked away on my tiny planet, we hadn't known this kind of agony. People lived simple lives. It wasn't that they didn't hurt, but somehow this was so different I couldn't even recognize it as the same thing. These were emotions, they were wounds that would never be closed no matter how much time or help they got.

Or maybe that wasn't true. My guys were getting better every day they were out of Evander. Other Super Soldiers had.

I hit the ground, my knees aching for a second before I couldn't feel them anymore. There was just too much everything. I couldn't think. Tears flooded my eyes, for what, I didn't know. What wasn't I crying about seemed more accurate. Everything was dark. Pain. Murder. Abuse.

Why did anyone bother trying? Why did any of us keep going when there was no point to any of it ever? Why? Just why?

I lost track of time. The ship tilted left and then right, or maybe it was me swaying. I'd lost my footing.

There just wouldn't be anything to...

Strong hands lifted me from behind. "Sienna, enough."

Trenton's voice reached me. I didn't know from where since it seemed like there was no reality anymore, just the edge of the universe where, in the end, everything was misery and destruction.

Blackness flooded my vision.

* * *

I woke up to the sounds of beeping and the whoosh of a medical machine. I was inside of one. Claustrophobia hit for a second before a cooling sensation flooded my body, and I closed my eyes, not caring one way or another whether I was inside a tube or for how long I'd have to stay there. Sleep was a balm I was glad to take however it came.

The next time I roused, I was in a bed. It was soft beneath me and the room quiet. I opened my eyes, and the sound of shuffling greeted me. Corbin stared down at me, a furrow to his brow, before he climbed into the bed and scooted us both around until he had his arms around my waist and my head on his chest. I nestled down into him, glad for his presence in the cold, cold world.

He smelled like coffee. Did Super Soldiers drink coffee? I'd never seen them have a cup.

Corbin stroked my back, gently. "How are you doing, Sienna?"

Not well. I closed my eyes without answering him, knowing I wouldn't sleep. I hadn't given any thought to the aftermath of what I'd done, just that I had done it. I needed to take down our captors to give Trenton the chance to take control of the ship and hope that the others woke up and could help. Clearly that had happened, or some version of it, or I'd not be lying here now with Corbin.

"Hurts." I didn't mean physically. My body felt fine. I wasn't even sure why I'd been in the med machine. It was just that I was so bone-tired and yet wide awake, so weary and yet... not at the same time. I didn't know how I was ever going to come out of this.

He stroked my hair. "I bet."

I managed to pick up my wrist. The level read nine. That wasn't good, but I couldn't even bring myself to care. I had no feelings left of my own, just the ability to somehow process all the ones I'd ingested.

"Wade wants to put you back into cryo for a while, get those numbers down. We tried the med machine but, as before, there is nothing we can do in there. We had hoped the machines here, since they're Evander made, might have some of the cures. They don't."

I closed my eyes. That just figured. Nothing anyone could do. "I don't want to go into cryo and wake up to a new world, new people, with no idea who anyone is. I don't think I can start over like that again and again."

He kissed my forehead. "I wouldn't let that happen to you. None of us would."

That was sweet, but I'd long ago learned that things happened whether anyone intended them to or not. "Are you okay?"

"Me? Sure, that fucking ray they used on us to take us down really sucked, but we fought back from it pretty well until we couldn't anymore. I'm going to figure out how to get resistance to it. That'll be my main task for the next however long it takes. Thanks for getting us out of cryo." He stopped his hand stroking. "Even if we'd all have preferred you didn't almost sacrifice yourself in the meantime."

I closed my eyes. They just felt too heavy to keep open even though I wasn't going to sleep. "I can only do what I can do. I'm not strong like all of you, or capable with the ship. I don't know how to do much of anything, but I have these two things I can do. I won't be any less than any of you. If I need to use my skills to save you, that's what I'll do."

He made a sound that didn't seem happy, but I wasn't going to lift my lids to get his facial expression. I just couldn't. "Are we going back for Artemis?"

"No need. She's on this vessel. We are bringing the whole thing, Artemis included, back to Mars Station to regroup. Our mission objective is done, thanks to you. We have the Evander ship and the Evander people who were left on this side of the galaxy all in cryo. This was what we wanted."

That made me open my eyes. "That's good news, right?"

I really needed some good news right now. In a major way.

"It is. So now we just need to figure out what to do next." He ran his hand over my wrist where my indicators were. Aha, I understood. They had to decide how they were going to make me healthy.

I leaned on my elbow and stared down at him. "Corbin, level with me. Wade is worried that I'm at a nine, isn't he?"

"Worried doesn't begin to cover how we all feel about it. Yes. But he's going to get the best possible help in healing you. So try not to worry."

I nodded. "I'm not sure I could worry right now. I'm

having trouble feeling anything through the... awful that's inside of me right now."

He ran his finger down the slope of my nose. "That'll pass. I promise."

I wished I could have Corbin's faith in that. I absolutely did not.

WHEN I FINALLY COULD MUSTER UP ENOUGH energy to leave the room with Corbin, it was to go to the glass enclosure where I had left Wade. I was getting a little bit too close to being infectious to Trenton and Wade. I had to stay away. Technically, it would need to be at ten for me to make them sick, but there was every reason to think the number would continue to rise, and we didn't want to find out it had happened after the fact.

Corbin, however, shut himself in the glass room with me as though he meant to stay.

I lifted an eyebrow but said nothing to him. He shook his head. "I'm not leaving, Sienna. I'm a Super Soldier. I don't believe you can make me sick."

I wasn't sure that was true. "We don't know that."

Wade walked into the other room. I hadn't seen anyone else yet, and it was strange to be on this ship without Evander running around. Not that I'd been here very long, but the ship itself seemed like it was coated in the essence of Evander. I hated this place.

"I don't want to go back in cryo." I hoped Wade could hear me through the glass.

He tilted his head. "I'm glad to see you, too."

I winced. He was right. That had not been the nicest greeting. I wasn't myself, and I didn't know if I'd ever be again. "Sorry."

He nodded. "You know, if you wanted to kill yourself, there are easier ways."

Corbin groaned. "He's a little bit upset with you. Took beautiful care of you once he roused from the stupor he was in. Make no mistake. Wade is in love with you, same as the rest of us, but you scared the shit out of him while he was locked in this room."

I'd known that was a factor, and I'd done it anyway. Rage flooded my system, and it was mean, not to mention misdirected. Even understanding all of that, I couldn't keep my mouth shut. I shouted at Wade through the glass. "I'd do it again."

"I know you would." He wasn't backing down on this, holding my gaze like he was ready to go round for round with me if that was what I was going to do.

Corbin sighed. "Come on now. This isn't helpful."

I rounded on him. He was even closer than Wade. "Don't tell me what to do. Everyone is always telling me what to do."

The door to the med bay opened and Blaze strode in, followed by Devil. They would've already know what was happening. The way they could hear everything, know everything, it was akin to the problems I'd had with Evander's Super Soldiers. There was no such thing as privacy.

"That must be some noise in your head." Dev walked toward me, and Blaze winced. He probably wouldn't have said that to me, or at least not like that.

They stood side-by-side, staring at me through the glass. I was suddenly reminded of the time the space-faring zoo had arrived on our planet. For twenty-four hours, we'd observed animals we'd never seen in our lives through glass cages. They hadn't stayed long because the authorities were after the owners for some kind of credits they owed. Still, I'd been sad for the animals trapped inside the cages, and I'd left early.

In that moment, I was the animal in the cage.

I pounded on the glass. "Keep staring. Better yet, go get your tablets and take a picture of me. It'll last longer."

Dev and Blaze stared at each other for a moment before they both looked at Wade. He shook his head. The silent communication was going to make me nuts. I paced to the other side of the enclosure, having to move around Corbin.

Wade shook his head. "Corbin, I'd prefer if you would come out of there. We can't be sure she can't make you sick."

My stomach dropped. I wouldn't be responsible for him dying. I pointed to the door. "Out."

"I'm good. I don't get sick. Advanced genes and all that."

I leaned against the wall. "I just spent a huge amount of energy and received a lot of pain to keep you all safe. Do you think you could please not make that for naught by possibly getting sick when we could prevent that?"

The door opened and closed; Kellan and Anders entered, followed a second later by Trenton. I supposed I could ask who was flying the ship, but it always seemed to be some kind of remote thing they did by their tablet. At the very least, I trusted them not to leave the ship floating in space where we could get hurt.

If that was even possible. We'd beaten Evander, hadn't

we? I'd taken them down. There shouldn't be any more problems in that regard.

"Must be nice to be done with having to fight Evander?" I asked the room, not caring which one of them answered me. And Corbin still hadn't left the enclosure with me. I guessed he really wasn't going to, and I didn't have it in me to keep trying to make him.

Anders placed his hand on the glass, and it was so sweet I walked back so I could reach mine up to do the same. "Several of them got away. We had to all wake up. It was just Trenton trying to handle everything. But we have the ship, so it's mostly over."

I closed my eyes. "I did all that, and we didn't even win. How did they wake up so fast?"

"They were on the other side of the ship. Didn't get hit with the first effect, I think." Kellan sighed. He paced between Wade and the glass enclosure. "You have to fix this, Wade. I can hear she's not okay."

Trenton shook his head. "Kellan."

"I told you she wasn't going to be okay," Wade yelled at the top of his voice. It was such an un-Wade thing to do that it startled me. For a second, I stared wide-eyed at him while he slammed his hand down on the table. "She completely overexerted herself. It turns out that they gave her illnesses they were making to try to take down Super Soldiers, and I don't have the slightest idea how to fix that. I can't fix any of it. So, please, tell me again how I have to fix this, Kellan, because I am one hundred percent sure that I've just been lazy and not in the mood."

Sarcasm dripped from his voice, and he sounded so lost to himself that I couldn't help but feel like I should fix it. Like I should be responsible for making Wade feel better. But the truth was I'd done everything I could do to keep us alive, and I had nothing left to give. I was an empty jar, and the lid was closed.

I was sorry Wade was suffering, but that was as far as I could go.

Kellan lifted an eyebrow. "I wasn't suggesting..."

"No," Wade snapped, slamming his hand down on the table next to him. "You're more than suggesting. You're outright saying."

"Okay," Trenton yelled. He looked pale, not himself at all. I touched the glass. It was frustrating to be separated from all of them, but nevertheless, I shot Corbin a look. He needed to get away from me.

They all turned to stare at Trenton. He took a long deep breath. "She's sick." He looked over at me. "You're sick. I'm not going to speak about you like you're not here."

I nodded as I sank down to the floor, still near the glass. "Thanks."

"Welcome." He knelt down and touched the glass on the other side of where I sat as though we could feel each other through the glass. I wasn't sure I could feel anything at all. Even if we'd been skin-to-skin. A few seconds later, he turned around to regard all of them again. "Instead of yelling because we all feel like shit that we might be losing her, let's strategize about what we can do about it."

I sighed. "Aren't we on the ship that can do something about it? This is an Evander vessel. I haven't seen others that I remember, but this one seems pretty big and substantial to me. Why aren't the cures here?"

Blaze shook his head. "They don't bother with things like that on vessels that transport Super Soldiers. We're expendable cargo. They can always make more of us. They have an abundance. They'd have that kind of thing on the ships that transfer the board of directors."

Wade sighed, some of his anger deflating. "That's not entirely true. I don't have all the details, but I know that Ari and some of the others found a cure for Waverly once on a random ship. They must have gotten smarter since then and removed the stuff. I'm sure that was true, once, Blaze, the way you knew it."

"Then what do we do?" Kellan looked around, making eye contact with everyone but me.

I'd had enough. I pounded on the glass. "Maybe *we* die." I rolled my eyes. Yes, I'd become the brat I never was, but it was as though I couldn't get all of the pain out of my head. There was nothing but anger and sadness deep inside of me. I was lost to it. I might never find my way out. "Sorry, I meant I. Since I'm the only one here who will be dying."

Kellan shook his head. "Make no mistake, sweetheart, if you die, I'm going with you. Maybe in a big fucking explosion where I take out some fucker who deserves to die, but I'm not doing any of this without you."

Well... that was quite a statement. "Kellan."

"You should believe that true from all of us." Trenton nodded his head. "Okay. You heard what he just said. It's true."

Wade turned his back. "I can't do that. My brother and sister need me until they're eighteen. Even if they don't see me, they need a guardian on the books. It's better they don't see me. But that doesn't mean I wouldn't want to, Sienna. I would just have to delay."

This was all too awful for me to digest. "Guys, the sad truth here is that I'm sitting at a nine." I checked my wrist to make sure that it still said that. It absolutely did. Would I have preferred an eight? Yes. Was I glad it wasn't a ten? Fuck yes, I was. "I am probably going to..."

Kellan shook his head. "Don't say it, Sienna. Don't utter

the words, because I'm not sure I will be able to restrain from breaking this glass and hauling you through the black hole if you do."

Wade spun around. "What?"

"Breaking the glass..."

The doctor waved his hand. "Not that. No, the other part. Hauling her through the black hole. That's a great idea."

Was it? I got to my feet, and Corbin came to stand right next to me. Kellan had caught all our attention. Could we actually go through the black hole? It was closed. They'd told me that on Mars Station. It had been shut down to stop Evander from coming back through. Could we just open it because we wanted to?

"Can you get it open?"

Kellan nodded. "I can get it open. I know how Wes closed it. He'd been trying for years. This last attempt worked. But, yes, I could break through." He pointed at his head. "Remember? I'm really smart."

I smiled. It was the first time I'd felt like it since I'd woken up. Kellan had lots of insecurities but not about his rather impressive IQ. "Oh, yes, I'd never forget."

He rocked back on his heels. "Good."

My amusement faded fast, and a headache in the center of my forehead took its place. That couldn't be a good sign. Or maybe it was about the emotions still. If the numbers on my arm were any indication, they were all related. My stress levels raised my viral load, and in turn I got sicker, which made me more stressed. It was really fun. Sarcasm in my own mind was never a healthy thing.

"So you could do it." Wade nodded. "And Trenton could navigate the hole. Blaze, do you think you could use your connection with Sterling, Canyon, or Rohan to get hooked up to however it is that they control time?" Wade held up his hand. "Yes, I know more about that than I'm letting on because I don't want to deal with it right now."

"What does that mean?" They might all understand what they were talking about, but I certainly didn't.

"Time travel." Corbin shrugged. "Worst kept secret lately. No one knows. But we do. Because we can hear things. Seems like Wade knows." He looked at Trenton. "Did you?"

He sighed. "I did. They have this secret building on The Farm. Ari was always running in and out of it. Never mind. Yes, I knew."

Time travel? That seemed as foreign a concept as I could perceive, but then again it had been days—weeks? who knew anymore—since they'd woken me, and I couldn't use the lights on Artemis. So perhaps this wasn't such a strange thing as I thought it was. Okay, I was putting that in a box to deal with later in the back of my mind. Everything was awful. I couldn't fathom time travel. It was probably a world ending disaster.

I hated my own internal thoughts. It was as though my mind lied to me. How long was this going to last? I couldn't focus on things, and they involved me. I had to try to stay present. Why was that so hard?

"We get through the black hole back to when they made the diseases she's sick with. The ones that were meant to make us sick. Of the same ilk as the device they used to take us down on the planet. And we cure her." Blaze spoke, and all eyes were on him. He was quiet, but there was never any question that he was in charge. It was like he listened thoroughly before he made any decisions, and he spoke only when he'd made one. He also had a temper, but he'd yanked it back so that I never saw it anymore. I was glad to be off his I-don't-trust-her list. That hadn't been a fun place to be.

Of course, I was in such a dour place he might put me back on it just because he couldn't stand to have me around. I pressed my forehead against the glass and closed my eyes. Maybe I could sleep through this whole thing. Was that possible? But not in cryo because that could go on indefinitely, and I could wake up when these guys were all dead and I had to talk to their grandsons. I groaned. No, please, not that. That meant they all had lives, and I had...

Corbin touched my arm. "Sienna? You okay?"

"Not even a little bit."

He drew me to him, his warmth nice even though I knew I might be killing him. "You have to let me go."

When he didn't answer, Blaze finally tilted his head. Some sort of silent communication must have happened because Corbin let go and stepped toward the door. "Only because they'll need me to keep you alive. If I'm sick, I'm draining resources from you. I don't want that."

Whatever it took for him to stay safe. Blaze shifted his stance, regarding Kellan again. "They closed it down to keep this side of the universe safe. I have no problem sacrificing everyone for Sienna, but she hasn't even been willing to let us put ourselves at risk to help her. Hated every second of it, and I'm not going to lose her when this is over because we've done something she considers unforgivable."

Trenton smirked. "Blaze, I think your EQ is rising."

The leader ignored him. I should be feeling grateful and relieved. I knew that. But there was the whole pit-of-blackness-around-my-soul problem at the moment.

Blaze rolled his eyes and spoke again to Kellan. "We need to time this so there is no chance of Evander coming with us or getting out."

Kellan spoke up. "That's where I come in. Well, Corbin and me. We can see to that happening."

"We're not ready." Dev spoke slowly. "Can't do it in this monstrosity of a ship. We have to drop off the sleeping beauties to Mars Station. Pick up supplies for Artemis. If I recall the specs correctly from my time with the Chen Empire, they were trying to make it work for Tommy Sandler's ships and not having a great time of it. The only ship that has ever successfully hooked up Wes' time controller is Artemis."

Trenton grinned. "Then I guess it's a good thing we have Artemis. I'll get going fixing her."

"We'll need help on Mars Station, but that's too risky. How close are we to The Farm?" Blaze asked.

Dev picked up his tablet. "Closer. Hours."

"Great. That's where we'll go. We'll drop off the Evander prisoners at The Farm. Diana can deal with her mother if they want them on Mars Station. That's not our problem." He snapped his fingers. "Wade, I know you want other doctors to look at her. Ari is there. Cash. And what's his face?"

Wade smiled. "Picking up expressions, too. The other doctor is Lewis. I might like Amber and Dane, too, but we'll never get all of them. So, yes. The Farm will work to get this done. We'll steal the device from The Farm. Devil?"

He nodded. "That's my job."

Blaze seemed settled in his decision. "Okay, then we have to understand that we're all lying. Every single one of us will be lying when we get there. We get Artemis fixed. Pick up supplies. Without anyone there hearing a single thing of truth. We don't say a word. There are three Super Soldiers who are just as good at it as we are. They tried to hide this, and we still found out. Not one word." He spun around to regard me. "Can you do that, love?"

"I don't know any of them. I'm not sure why I would ever consider telling them anything. But I don't want anyone hurt." I was like a constant repeated recording with that subject, but there it was. "So we can't open it if anyone gets hurt."

Anders cleared his throat. "You can trust us to manage that. We won't put this quadrant in danger. I promise you that. And I'll even shoot Wes a message on our way through, telling him he doesn't have to let us back in if he doesn't want to."

I had a pretty good idea that wasn't going to happen. There was a small chance this was going to work. I knew that, and I didn't have the smallest idea of battle strategy or anything related. What were the chances that I was even going to make it to the other side of the galaxy? How long of a trip was it?

"Wade? Do I make it that far?" I needed the truth from him, and I wished I were a Super Soldier who could hear his heartbeat and somehow know what that meant. Was he lying? Appeasing me? I might be able to read his face if I was in better shape. But now they all just looked and seemed angry and sad. "Tell me."

Maybe I was better than I thought, because I was actually able to watch the emotions cross over his face. A million of them. He might have lied to me, and then he thought better of it. Wade cleared his throat. "You might have to go under cryo, my love."

Okay. They kept bringing it up, and I was going to have to deal with it. I couldn't continue to say "no, no, no" just because I didn't like the idea. I was either telling him to let me die, or I was telling him to put me under and try to fix me again, however long it took. Or maybe there was a tweak to that.

"There has to be an end date."

He understood me, because he nodded, but Trenton looked between us. "Explain?"

"I'm not living endlessly in cryo. There's a date when enough is enough." If I had to live in a glass cage or in cryogenic sleep, I wasn't going to do it forever.

He snorted. "Well, obviously. The end date is that we get the cure. We cure you. There is a very close end date. A year, maybe. You can hold out that long or go in cryo. There's a not so distant end date."

Enough. "Really? You want to do it?" I snapped. It was beneath me, but I'd been selfless, and now I was paying the price for it mentally. I'd apologize later when I actually felt sorry.

"I would do it, Sienna, if I could. I would gladly take it from you in a heartbeat."

Yep, I was the worst. Sorry didn't take long to feel. "I'm... Trenton you didn't deserve that. I'm not right."

"We know that." He knocked on the glass. "We're all in love with you. Hands down done without you. And I know pain and loss. I'm not doing it again. I had revenge to fuel me before. This time, I'm with Kellan. If you're out, I'm out. So try to hang on as long as you can. We're not going to let this be endless for any of us."

The responsibility of this was staggering. It stole my breath and rendered my already confused thoughts silent. I didn't want anyone hurt and that included them all deciding to go on some blaze of righteous glory on my behalf. I had been raised to help people. How would I live with myself if it all went wrong for those I actually loved?

Well, I guessed I wouldn't live with myself. I'd actually be dead.

Darkness was this life. I closed my eyes. There it went

again. Other people's crap crowding out my own thoughts as though all the goodness everywhere had been sucked away.

"Okay. I'll trust you."

Blaze smiled. "Good. We're going to move a bed in there and make sure you're all comfortable. It's not a jail cell. It's a temporary holding until we get that number down just a little." He turned and then stopped. "Sienna, thank you for what you did."

I swallowed, tears threatening my eyes. "You're welcome. Of course."

"If you do something like that again, I'm going to let Devil paddle your ass."

Dev jolted. "How did I become the one to paddle her ass? You want to do that, have at it. I'm not the one dishing out punishments. You're the leader, oh masterful one."

Blaze threw his head back and laughed. It was a bright, delighted sound that I wished I could appreciate. I wished I could feel the humor in this moment, to even know what was funny anymore. Laughing was one of those things that made life worth living. Without it, what was the use of any of it?

"I don't get it either." Anders shrugged and winked at me. "If anyone is going to be paddling your ass, you know it's going to be Trenton."

He held up his hands. "You boys keep your kinky to yourselves. I've got my own set of happy. And I promise you, if I did that, she wouldn't think of it as a punishment."

All of this was lost on me. It was a damned shame.

THINGS WERE PRETTY quiet after that. The guys scampered off, and eventually I drifted off to sleep on the bed that Anders dragged in. It was quiet in the med bay, and I slept very well until I heard footsteps approaching. I sat up, my heart in my throat. I'd assumed the ship was safe, but what if it weren't. What if...

My fears proved to be for naught. It was Kellan. He walked toward the glass and sat down on the other side of it, smiling at me. Smiling wasn't Kellan's natural facial expression. I was touched that he made the effort for me or that he even wanted to. Maybe my mood was slightly better.

"Hey," I whispered. We were alone, and I wasn't sure it was the middle of the night, but it felt like it was on my body clock, so I treated it that way.

He tapped on the glass. "I was hoping not to wake you."

"I'm a light sleeper."

Kellan nodded. "I can see that." He actually yawned. "Sorry, cryo throws me off. I'm going to be on and off tired for a bit. Not great for a Super Soldier when we're expected to wake up and fight like nothing happened to us."

"Maybe the expectations were unreasonable, not your reaction to cryo."

He leaned his head on the glass. "What is your number right now?"

I looked down at my wrist. "No change."

Kellan put a finger to his mouth like he wanted me to be quiet before he rose and entered my enclosure. I pointed my finger at him. He wasn't supposed to come in here. If Wade came out of the office, he was going to yell at him. But then again, Wade was probably asleep since he'd been in that other room for a long time. I hoped he was. This was a lot.

He lay down next to me on the bed. I should tell him to go. This was ridiculous. But I wanted to curl up against him. I had to control myself. If I hit ten tonight, he'd be in danger of catching something, and there was no amount of cuddling that was worth that. How could we cuddle in the future if he got sick? Of course, I might not have a future to cuddle.

Picking up my wrist, he kissed it right over the number. The gentlest of caresses. I sighed. Okay. He could stay for a minute. That was fine, just a minute. Or two. We kept having this conversation, over and over. How much of what I wanted went against their personal ability to make decisions?

No, I was right on this. I rolled over to tell him to get out of my bed, but his eyes were closed, and he looked so peaceful. Kellan never looked this relaxed. I would wake him in a second. For just now, I'd watch him sleep because he'd crawled in here even though he'd known he wasn't supposed to in order to just sleep.

I reached out and stroked the side of his face gently. If it woke him, I'd kick him out, but he didn't stir. He was a Super Soldier. That would wake him if he wanted to be woken. That had to be hard. They never could really deeply sleep unless they were drugged into cryo to do so. I knew their genes had been manipulated, but didn't they need REM like the rest of us?

Dropping my hand, I snuggled back down. If he was pretending to not wake up so that I'd let him rest, I'd give him an A for performance technique. That was something I'd never seen, a theater show. Did people still do that?

He smelled fresh, like he'd just showered. The scent of a cinnamon soap on him was different than usual for Kellan. He probably had to use whatever was on this ship. I could use a shower myself. With their scent of smell so heightened, did they know when I smelled bad even before I did?

That was sort of a gross thing to think about.

I wasn't going to go there in my head. They must think I was okay, or they wouldn't all want to be close to me. I was going to go with that.

Closing my eyes, I made a decision. I was just going to go with it. For once in this strange, bizarre life where I was constantly between what was happening to me and what I wanted, I would take what I wanted. In this moment, even if it was insanely wrong, I wanted this.

I didn't know how long I slept, but I woke up when Wade banged on the window. "Hey, tough guy, you know you're not supposed to be in there. I'd really appreciate it if you guys wouldn't get yourself sick so I have to figure out how to save you, too."

Kellan groaned but sat up. "Looks like we got caught. We made it longer than I thought we would. Wade must have been sleeping."

I stared at Kellan for a second while my mind cleared. "Were you awake when I thought you might be awake?"

He shrugged. "Half awake."

"You're always half awake, I think."

Kellan got up and rubbed his eyes. "How would I know the difference?"

That was a perfectly legitimate question. He'd never had the difference. How would he know? I swung my legs over the side of the bed. "How long until we're at The Farm?"

"We're there." Kellan knew the answer even though he'd been asleep, too. I looked down at my wrist. If I were at ten, I was never going to forgive myself for being so selfish for the hours I'd taken. My head was clearer than before. I could only hear a thousand souls yelling in pain in my head, as opposed to the ten thousand the day before. It wasn't that many. There were only a hundred or so on the ship when I took on their pain. But it felt that way. My number was at eight. It had lowered a touch. I let out a breath and held up my arm so Wade could see it through the glass. He nodded, and the relief in his gaze must have been mirroring my own.

"That's good that we're there." I really did need that shower. "Do you think they'll let me take a bath when we're there? Before they start poking and prodding at me, and I say nothing about what we're doing?"

Wade snorted. He smiled as he spoke. That was a nice sight. Different from earlier. "I think they'll let you take a shower. This isn't going to be a prison thing."

Blaze entered and Wade spoke to him over his shoulder. "She's down a notch."

"Good, maybe Kellan sneaking off to sleep with her was some magic touch."

Kellan groaned as he exited the enclosure. "He wants you to know we didn't get away with it, Sienna. Just in case we thought we were sneaky, Blaze already knew."

"I know most things," Blaze responded with a shrug. "And then sometimes I don't know anything."

That seemed like a pretty accurate description for my life as well. Although, lately I wasn't sure that I knew anything at all.

* * *

The approach to The Farm was beautiful. We'd landed the whole ship where we'd been met by more people ready to come on board and help than I could have imagined. The guys were all instantly busy. Blaze had to report in to some people I recognized from the meeting on Mars Station about what had happened, and the others scattered away to go see various people who could help them in some way. Of course, they were all lying. We weren't there because we wanted to tell our story.

With nothing to do and no direction as to where I was supposed to go, I stood and observed while some big machines pulled Artemis out of the ship and loaded her into a large hangar that I could see in the distance. Since we needed Artemis healthy to use her the way we had to, we would be here on The Farm just as long as it took for that to happen.

"Hello," a voice called out to me, and I jumped, my hand going to my throat in reflex. It took me a second to remember Diana from the brief lunch I'd had with her. She was tiny, dark-haired, and smart. Or at least that had been my initial impressions. The women who I'd been with were all close to one another. As the outsider in a formed group, it was hard to know what was real and what I'd picked up from other people's perceptions.

I smiled. "Hi. Am I in the way here? I suppose I should

go inside and figure out where I was supposed to be." Which was a polite way of me not saying I needed to shower. That was one of those things maybe I didn't say aloud in front of strangers. Plus, there was the other factor. As a person who was sick enough to stay in a glass cage the night before, I should probably not have been wandering. Of course, I was at eight now. There was a huge difference in eight to nine. At least in as much as the guys had all relaxed when they'd seen or heard it. Perhaps it was just a question of my own ability to heal. If I could get back down to eight, I was maybe not as dire as they'd worried.

Maybe was the keyword.

"No, I don't see why you would be. They're all inside making arrangements for you. I know you didn't like that last time. Or at least that's what I heard. I wanted to make sure you knew."

I smiled at her. "Things are a little different now."

"Funny how that goes. I only have one Super Soldier to contend with. You have five. That has to be a lot. Plus Wade and Trenton have strong personalities."

I opened and closed my mouth. "I think I'm a lot to deal with. More so than any of them. I'm sick and in constant danger to myself and others. I can do weird things with my mind that make me sought after by bad people. I probably got my family killed. I think if anything, they're dealing with a lot in me."

She smiled slowly. "I think my husbands are dealing with a lot in me, too. I like you. You're a little disgruntled. I am, too. You just express it better. I think we're going to be very close friends."

I blinked. Really? She had gotten that from what I said? "Um, sure, sounds good."

Were friendships made just like that? "Come on. Two

of my husbands are going to want to check you out medically, and that'll be no fun. You might as well have something delicious to eat before that happens."

My stomach grumbled, but I had a more pressing concern. "I could really use a shower."

"That's easy. I'm going to bring you to Waverly's. They'll find you there, your guys, as soon as they realize you aren't where they left you, which will be very fast. Look." She pointed, and I followed her indication to where Anders appeared in the distance. "He's already figured out that you're moving, and he's watching."

She was better at this than me. How had she spotted him so fast? "I wasn't worried. They take very good care of me."

"We're lucky in that."

It was great to hear it expressed that way. "When you don't have anyone to care about you for a long time, it is really infectious in the best possible way to be wrapped up in it now."

I was feeling better already. Diana was direct, a little quirky, and a bottle of positive energy. I could really get used to her company.

She brightened up. "Yep, good friends."

On Mars Station I wouldn't have imagined that possible. Things had altered, and I couldn't say I was the least bit upset about it. I had a new friend. It was tentative, and I liked the feeling, a lot.

Waverly's house was a distance away, but I could tell immediately why Diana brought me there. It was an actual house, like the ones we'd had on our planet, not a military encampment where people lived. Of course, any security The Farm had probably didn't extend this far out. Still, I could see why she would have chosen this, despite the risk.

This felt more like living and less like simply existing. This was why I hadn't liked Mars Station. I wanted real, not made to be a replica of it.

The owners weren't home, but Diana entered like she had every right to do so. I hoped that was the case and Waverly and her husbands weren't going to object to us just barging in. I gave up worrying about that in the shower. It was warm, and I decided that I could stand there all day without needing anything else. Of course, I wasn't going to do that. I'd never been anywhere where water wasn't a problem. I had to be cognizant not to overuse supplies. So when I could tear myself away from the comfort, I turned off the spray and wrapped myself in one of the towels that was neatly stacked next to the door.

As I dried off, I noticed that Diana must have left a change of clothes for me, too, and I quickly dressed, glad not to have to put on the same thing I'd been wearing since we got attacked on the planet. Was that just days ago? It felt like a lifetime.

I stepped back into the hallway and caught the sound of voices downstairs. Waverly stood at the bottom of the stairway and smiled warmly as I approached.

"Sienna, I'm so glad you're here."

All eyes were suddenly on me, and I was glad to see that Trenton was among those waiting.

"Thank you for letting me clean up here. It was a real treat."

She waved her hand. "It's nothing. What's mine is yours. How are you feeling?"

A blond man stepped up next to her, and as I approached, he watched me with kind eyes. "Would you mind if I looked at your wrist? I'm a doctor."

I met Trenton's gaze, and he nodded. Not that I thought

anyone would lie about that, but when everyone was a stranger in a universe where few could be trusted, it was nice to have the support.

"Ari and I have known each other a long time." Trenton crossed to me and put his hand on my shoulder just as I held out my arm for Ari. Maybe we could get this fixed so I never had to deal with doctors again. I'd just be fixed. I almost jolted at the peak of optimism coming back in my head. If my whole life were an experiment, then perhaps I was learning how long it would take for me to come back from a huge event like the one I'd had on the Evander ship.

Ari nodded. "So eight isn't a great number, but it's better than nine." He dropped my arm. "Wade is really upset that you got to nine. But we'll just say that eight is improvement and feel good about that. He also told me that you literally took down a ship of Super Soldiers by taking on everyone's pain. I can't say that I one hundred percent understand that. I mean, the science of it. I'm thinking the women on your planet must have some extreme action in your frontal cortexes and—"

Waverly interrupted him. "Ari."

"Right, sorry. The why of it can wait. You are not a science project for me to figure out. I'm much more interested in how you're feeling now. Emotionally. I'm not sure I'd be standing straight."

Trenton sighed. "Before they eliminated psychiatry as not necessary in our society, that is what Ari did. He really does care about how you're feeling."

"That's kind of you." But there were a lot of eyes on me right then. "I'm not really comfortable talking about myself, and these circumstances make it even worse."

"Then we're going to eat," Waverly called out, and everyone turned and headed toward the kitchen.

Trenton nodded to me. "Hungry?"

As it turned out, I was obscenely hungry. Ravishingly famished. Everyone was quickly introduced, and I realized I had met most of them the last time I was around them. It was just hard to keep track of new people, but I quickly caught up. Waverly had four husbands: Canyon and Rohan —they were both Super Soldiers—and also Jackson and Ari, who were not. Diana had five: Damian, Judge, Cash, Lewis and Sterling. The last was a Super Soldier, the others were not.

My guys eventually filed in. Although The Farm had a huge amount of people on it, the gathering made it seem like there were family groups of people that got together within the larger group itself.

Maybe that was what we were all looking for when it came down to it, a group that we could call our own that helped us have a sense of community in a universe that was more interested in letting us float off into oblivion if we weren't careful.

"How many do you think got away?" Sterling asked Blaze, who was the last one to come in. "How many Evander soldiers are still running around out there?"

Blaze winced. "Not sure. I was pretty out of it. Like those flashes of light when you first wake up from cryo and you're not really there yet. That was then. Trenton would know better."

Next to me, Trenton stiffened. "I was mostly concerned with Sienna and getting her out of there safely."

Sterling held up his hands. "You guys brought down the Evander vessel and took prisoner most of the men who are now sleeping peacefully in cryo. I'm not here to judge. I'm just trying to get a sense of how many people we have to worry about showing up. Planning, that's it."

There was tension between Blaze and Sterling. I looked between them when Diana spoke fast. "You're right, Sienna. They don't get along. Old baggage that maybe someday they'll make peace with."

I hadn't spoken aloud. Did Diana have some mind reading ability?

"I read it on your face. Just thought you might want to know you were right."

Cash leaned over and kissed her cheek. "Might be one of those things you should have kept to yourself."

She frowned. "I never know exactly what I should and shouldn't say."

Damian shrugged. "Say anything you want as long as you keep talking."

There was a story in that, but I didn't want to ask it right now. Instead, I focused on what Diana had said earlier. "I'm sure if they don't get along, there's a reason. Blaze is one of the best people I know."

To my surprise, Sterling grinned. "Well, look at you, Blaze. She has your back in a major way. Never thought I'd see the day when the Commander would be hooked like you are. Good for you. It makes us human."

"We were already human." Blaze took a long drink of his water. "We just didn't know it."

Canyon picked up his drink and held it toward Blaze in a toast. "Cheers to that."

The rest of the night went more smoothly. It was pretty much congenial, and despite having slept with Kellan for however long, by the end of dinner, I was yawning. Devil pushed his chair back and walked over to me.

"Come on. Let's get you to bed."

That sounded great. I just had no idea where that was. "Where am I staying?"

"We have rooms. In the main area. A family suite, as they call it. It's comfortable, and I set you up to make sure you would be happy there."

I rose from my seat. That meant a long walk back. It hadn't seemed like such a long trek on the way over to Waverly's house, but now on the return, I was going to feel every step. Still, I wouldn't complain. I'd set out to do what I said I would do. I got us off the Evander ship, and even though we now had to silently lie to get what we needed, we had a plan that had a chance of working.

On our way out the door, I met the gazes of each of my guys. They weren't any more comfortable than I was, and yet here we were in the thick of this. Maybe none of us would ever really know how to behave in these situations. It didn't matter. Our ability to fit in mattered the least out of everything we did or didn't do right now.

I'd never be the most popular girl in any room, and I didn't think I wanted to be.

Still, Diana grinned, and I did the same back to her.

"Thank you," I spoke to Waverly and Diana. They were being nothing but nice, and I couldn't let whatever it was that always made me feel separate from everyone else make me be rude. They were kind. I would be the same.

After we left, we might never see each other again. A pang of sadness hit me. I'd have liked to know these women, to understand what made them who they were and why they would take in a stranger, feed her, and make sure she was comfortable.

"Sienna." Waverly got to her feet. "If you need anything, I want you to know that however things seem now, Diana and I were both at one point lost in the universe. We did eventually figure out how to make our own homes. Yours can be here with us if that's what you want."

That was really, really nice of her to say that. "Thank you, Waverly."

We were outright lying to these people. And for the first time, that bothered me. When we left here, we were going to undo what they had done to keep us all safe. We were going to open the black hole and, like a pointed arrow, shoot ourselves right at Evander until we could fix what they'd done to me.

Devil squeezed my hand. If he knew my thoughts, he didn't say.

Wade cleared his throat. "Check your number before you go to bed. If it's back to nine, please let me know."

"I will." Devil tugged me toward him, and we left the dinner.

The sun was setting outside, and it cast an orange glow on this strange planet. I shivered. Without the sun, it had gotten colder. Without a word about it, Dev pulled off his coat and wrapped me up in it. I looked like a child wearing my father's clothing, that was how huge it was on me.

"So, how well did you know the Super Soldiers here?"

He sighed. "Well enough. As well as I knew anyone. I was not the person they wanted to be around. I was a rough commander. I believed in getting the job done no matter how we did that. To be fair, I had a pretty good track record for not getting my men killed."

That was something. An important something. "Blaze seemed very tense."

I could keep quiet about it, but everyone else knew what was going on. If they were eavesdropping, I doubted they'd get any new information from listening to me. Dev was quiet. I wondered if he'd answer me, and finally, he did.

"Canyon and Rohan let Blaze think they were dead. Sterling? I don't know all the details. But I think he's angry at them, and they don't like it. I don't know. I don't really care. I only care about what the rest of us will do from here. Not what mistakes we made back when we didn't know better." He paused. "Sienna, I really only care about you."

THE ROOMS TURNED out to be very comfortable. Very similar in a lot of ways to the rooms I'd had in the temple back home. They were small, with nothing special about them, but still we'd be comfortable. There were eight beds amongst the three bedrooms, with a main room and a bathroom. I supposed if we were going to spend any real time here, then I'd decorate it in some way like I had at home. Small touches of things that I could find and liked.

I bet people had done that here.

I looked around. "Where should I sleep?"

If Dev had arranged this, then I imagined he had a sense of how things were supposed to go. He pointed left, and I went into the room that had the biggest bed. In fact, it was the only one with a solo bed in the room. The others had two and one had three, which meant two of them would sometimes be bunking in the main room. But that was neither here nor there at the moment. I caught on pretty quickly with what he was thinking.

"I get this room and one of you stays with me?" I touched the bed. It was scratchy, but I wasn't going to complain. Anything halfway soft would do after the bed in the med bay. My wrist still said eight, and as long as I didn't inch up to nine, I supposed I wouldn't have to go into the med bay here.

"If that's okay. It also allows you to say no to any of us and be alone. It occurred to me that you've had very little ability to have privacy in a long time. You might like to sometimes be alone."

I almost asked him how long we'd be here, but that was a problem question. Arguably, if we weren't about to rob this place of its time thingy, then we would likely stay a while for sure. I ran a hand through my hair. "That's thoughtful of you."

"I occasionally have my moments." His self-deprecating smile was adorable and the first time I'd seen it on Dev. I reached out and stroked my finger over his mouth, and as his smile died, heat in his gaze took its place.

Devil and I had happened fast. One second, I had been afraid of him, the next tentatively trusting him, and then— bam—he had been one of mine. But maybe that was some- times how things went. The urgency of them, the rightness settling fast until you just instantly knew that it was right even if it was senseless and sort of impossible. I had little time. Truth was, I was dying. Everyone knew it, and they might be trying to reverse time and space for me to undo it, but there it was anyway.

It might be that nothing worked. That my time had been shortened by decades, and I could rail against it, or I could get on with living just as fast as I wanted to without having to understand it more than that.

"Just wanted to memorize what your smile felt like with my finger."

He brought my hand to his mouth and kissed the top of

it, holding it there for a long time. "On Earth, there are these things called movies."

I'd heard of them, even seen a few that came every once in a while to our planet. Everyone would run to witness the event, even those of us living in a temple. "Yes."

"And in them, sometimes, they put on shows like they're living in a different time. Old, pre-bombed times. Men were very polite, very restrained. It was a big deal to kiss a woman on her hand. I've wanted to do that with you since I first laid eyes on you. It just seemed like it would be appropriate to treat you like a lady from that time."

I went up on my tiptoes and kissed his mouth, gently. He tasted sweet, like the fruity dessert we'd just been eating. Dev closed his eyes and pressed back, his mouth surprisingly soft for a person who was as hard as him. He dropped my hand to cup my cheek, and I could have melted into him if such a thing were possible.

He pulled back but just to kiss me again for a long moment. When we broke apart, we both panted as though we'd run a race. Our mouths were still so close I could feel his warm breath against my face. I loved the intimacy of this moment.

"Sienna, did I do that okay?"

I didn't give him a second longer to feel insecure. This was a man who could kill in a heartbeat, but he wanted so much to be gentle with me. It was everything I needed, the lethal strength mixed with his sweet vulnerability. "You kiss like you were made to do it."

Dev scooped me up, not moving, just bringing me so that we were at eye level. I wrapped my legs around his waist, my arms around his neck.

"I was made to be a killer, but I am so glad that I get the privilege of kissing you."

I didn't think he was made to be a killer any more than any of us were actually made for any particular reason. But now wasn't the time for that sort of discussion. He'd brought me back here, and I wasn't fooling myself about what he was hoping we would do. I wanted the same in a major way.

My panties were already soaked, and all this man had done was kiss me twice.

He spun us around until he laid me down on the scratchy bed that suddenly didn't feel quite so bad on my skin. Or maybe it was just Devil making everything better. I wondered if anyone had ever told him that he had that effect on the world. "You being here... it just makes life so much lighter, so much brighter, so much more... everything good."

I didn't have the way with words that he did, although I doubted that mattered to him. When I said that, it was as though I'd lit a spark inside of Devil. He sucked in a long breath. "The fact that you could see me like that? The fact that I could mean that much to you when I shouldn't have the right to even touch you is just amazing. I don't know what I ever did to deserve this, but I promise you, Sienna, I will never take a second with you for granted. You will always get the very best from me. Every second that I breathe, it will be to honor you."

I eased back just enough to take off my shirt. I wanted to be exposed in front of him, for him to see all of me. What would it be like to be worshiped by Dev? I was about to find out, and wasn't I the luckiest person there ever was because of it.

He widened his eyes. "Your breasts."

I waited for him to say more, but that seemed to be all that he was going to get out. I grinned. That was sort of fun. I'd rendered Dev speechless. I wasn't bound up in undergarments like I usually was. Diana hadn't given me any, and I couldn't say at the moment that I cared very much. Better to be bare and let him see my skin. I swallowed, my breath catching in my throat.

"The way that you look at me—"

He interrupted. "I've never seen anything so beautiful. Tell me what you like, how you would like things to be. Teach me."

That was funny considering how little experience I had with this. But it was obviously more than he had. I ran my hand over my nipple, feeling a jolt when I did. I was so turned on that every touch seemed like a lot right now. "Suck on this."

Dev visibly swallowed before he leaned forward and did just as I asked. The pinch of pain had me gasp, and then I let my head fall backward. My neck could suddenly not support the weight of it, and besides, I wanted to do nothing but feel every second of the pleasure-slash-pain his beautiful mouth performed on my nipple right that second. He squirmed above me in a way that was so un-Devil. He wasn't a man who moved without a reason to do so. Devil was strong and steady. But I made him squirm, and that was amazing.

He lifted his head but only long enough to take the other nipple in his mouth. I cried out, this time knowing the pinch that would come made the anticipation half the fun of it. He squeezed my other breast, hard. Dev took direction well, and just one instruction had told him I wanted it a little bit rough from him. Now, it was my turn to squirm. I needed my hands busy, or I was going to lose my mind.

This was as much about giving as taking from me. I tugged at his shirt and threw it aside. He was big, maybe the broadest out of all the guys, and his muscles were defined as though he'd been sculpted from stone. All hard lines everywhere. He was also scarred, badly.

Crisscrossing marks that looked like he'd been clawed by an animal marred his skin. It was hard to scar a Super Soldier. That much I knew. What had done this to him? He pulled back, watching my reaction as I let my gaze caress him before I touched one of the marks. "What did this to you?"

"An animal." He sighed. "I put myself between one and my men. Years ago. I thought I was done for. A big cat. Huge. We got too close to its babies, but Evander expected us to perform. I expected to be dead. No idea why they didn't just let me die. But I got to have this moment, so I'll be grateful." He looked away suddenly. "Ugly?"

There was no part of him that was ugly. "Not at all. You should know how striking you are, but if you don't, let me tell you. You're really handsome, and I'm glad the cat didn't kill you. You make everything better."

I'd say that as many times as he needed to hear it.

"I like how you see me even if you're the only one in the universe who can view what you do." He pushed me back down again onto the bed. It bounced slightly from our weight. We tore at each other's clothes, Devil literally. While it was sort of funny that I clawed at his pants, he actually managed to tear mine to shreds.

I giggled, and he stopped. "Did I do something wrong?"

I shook my head, rolling him beneath me before I could overthink the act. "No. We just have to be careful. I don't have other clothes."

"I'll get you as many as you need. Fuck, I'll figure out how to make them myself if I need to."

The thing was, I believed him. He would if that were what I required. We were naked and he was gorgeous beneath me. I didn't know why I thought this would be better for him beneath me, but there was part of Dev that needed to be taken care of. I could see it every time I stared at him. Inside of Devil was a man not sure why he still existed in the universe. I wanted him to know just how much value he had to me, and how grateful I was that he'd decided he wanted to be one of mine.

"Don't move." I grinned. "Much."

I kissed down his body until I got to his cock. This was as new to me as it would be to him. I'd not done this before, but I imagined I could work it out. My confidence grew with every sigh he made, every twitch of his muscles as I simply kissed his skin. How much was he going to like what I did next?

I kissed the top of his cock, and it hardened. I smiled as that happened. There was the best sort of power in giving pleasure. It was my gift to give to him. My mouth watered, not sure what exactly would happen next but wanting every second of it just the same.

"You know someone was the first to do this." I spoke low, knowing he could hear me. "There was the first person out there who at some point said to themselves, I'd like to suck on that cock. And did."

He flared his nostrils. "Say that again."

I lifted an eyebrow. "Which part?" I wasn't going to recite the whole thing again.

"That word."

I knew which one he wanted. "Cock."

He nodded. "That's the one. I love the way it sounds coming out of your mouth."

"Cock. Cock. Cock." I sucked hard after I said the last one. Pleasure filled me at the same time it must have hit him. We both moaned. I moved my head up and down, struggling to take all of him but doing the best I could. He seemed to like it, and at the very least he wasn't complaining.

There was little to no noise around us except that which we made ourselves. His moans, my little sighs of pleasure. He tasted salty and male. I could get addicted to this. Dev needed to let me do this, a lot.

He pulled himself out of me, fast. I gasped. What was going on? Why had he done that?

"I know enough to know that I want to be inside of you, and before that, I want to feel you on the inside, Sienna. I need that more than anything. You can taste me, and so help me I can taste you."

"I..." Whatever I would have said stopped when he pushed my legs apart. His mouth was on me fast, kissing both of my thighs. I shuddered with anticipation. He'd never done this before, but I already knew he'd be an expert the second he touched me. This was Devil. He never failed.

He kissed my pussy, breathing me in when he did. Lifting his gaze, he met mine. My cheeks must've been bright red for how hot they felt. This was such a personal thing to do, and if I wasn't so transfixed, knowing what was about to happen, I might actually be embarrassed. I had no idea if that was normal for women to feel or not. My breath caught in my throat.

"You have no idea how much I am going to love this, Sienna."

I loved how my name sounded coming out of his mouth, and I had nothing to say in that moment because almost as soon as he'd said that, he put his tongue on me. At first, it tickled, but quickly that sensation stopped and was replaced by pure pleasure. I leaned back. I couldn't watch him, it was too much in that moment, but I could feel. Oh, by the universe, yes I could.

He found my clit and sucked on it, moaning when he did, his hips jerking into the bed. The noise was my undoing. I squirmed. This was so much. Every nerve ending in my body was on fire. I wasn't sure I could take anymore, almost wanting him to stop so I could breathe. But there was no halting this because the universe ceased to exist outside of what Dev was doing to me.

I exploded. Tears came to my eyes, as though I was releasing more than pleasure, and it made my body shake. My muscles vibrated of their own accord, and I couldn't make them stop, even if I'd had the wherewithal to try. He lifted his head and in a second was over me, kissing my mouth. It should have been weird to have him go straight from kissing my pussy to kissing my other lips, but it wasn't. It was hot. Everything Dev did was.

He kissed me slowly, as though he had every minute in the world. There was no rush in him right now even though the hardness of his cock must mean that he was in discomfort. But he acted like all he wanted to do was kiss me.

I cupped the side of his face. "You made me shaky. Thank you."

He smiled down at me. "You make me shudder, too."

I kissed him hard, increasing the pressure as he kissed me back. I wanted him inside of me. Pulling back, I met his steady gaze. Dev was hard everywhere. I reached between us and stroked his cock once. "I need more."

"Inside of you?" His voice was low, he sounded hoarse.

"Yes, please." I nodded. "Deep inside of me."

He did as I asked, shifting so he could push inside of me. I sighed with his entrance. This felt so much like he belonged inside of me. The pleasure built every second that he stayed still, filling me fully and not rushing to move again.

I squeezed him tightly between my legs, using my muscles to bring us both pleasure. He moaned, and it moved through me like he'd stroked my clit. I loved that he found so much pleasure with us being joined. It really made it like we were one in that moment.

Then he started to gently pull out before he pistoned back inside of me. The time for gentle was over, and oh yes, I loved this, too. I held on, taking this ride with him. Every jolt of his body made me cry out until I was practically shouting. I didn't even care. It just felt that good.

Over and over we ground against each other until I was sure that I was going to explode into a million pieces they'd never be able to put back together.

But when it happened, it was sweet, an easy surge that flooded me until I saw a white light in front of my vision. I caught my breath, bathing in the heaven of the whole thing. I drifted up, not sure I was going to come down. And that was okay. I'd be content to stay like this.

He spoke my name in my ear, and it sounded like he loved me. I'd never known my name could be that way.

But then again, everything about this man someone had named Devil seemed like love to me.

It just was. I didn't have to explain it. He was mine. He belonged with me.

* * *

I didn't remember falling asleep, but the loudest bang I'd ever heard roused me from my sleep. I gasped, coming to fast as Dev ripped me from the bed.

He'd been next to me. I knew that because it was as

though I could feel he'd been there, but he was out of the sheets faster than me. My head wasn't clear. I'd been out cold.

"What?"

He wrapped me in the sheet that we'd just had covering us. "Someone is attacking. Bombs."

The door flung open, and Trenton rushed in. He was shirtless. Dev threw on his underwear.

"Go. I've got her," Trenton said as he tugged me toward him.

"Yes." Devil ran from the room. They had obviously worked out something while I still didn't know what was going on.

"Who is bombing us?"

Trenton led me from the room. It seemed like it was just the two of us in here. That much I'd gathered fast. The door to one of the other rooms swung open, and one of the beds was unmade. The lights weren't on anywhere except in there, and I guessed that was where Trenton had been sleeping.

That changed fast, lights illuminating brightly while he dragged me and the sheet I was still wrapped in to a table in the corner.

"Come on. Under here."

He wanted me to get under the table? Wasn't there anything safer to do?

"Trenton?" I finally found my voice. "What is happening?"

He got under with me but only so he could place himself between me and the doorway. Finally, he answered me. "I don't know more than you do. The others would know. Well, not Wade. But the Super Soldiers would know. They're better out there. They'll get this under control. And you and I will stay under this table until we know it's safe, because I won't be losing you in an explosion."

He hugged me tight to him. We had no weapons on us, or at least I didn't think we did, and all we had was the table to protect us from the ceiling coming down on us. "Who would be attacking us? I thought... I thought the war was over now that we had Evander?"

"Fuck. I don't know. There's always someone to hate us, right? Maybe this is those few soldiers who got away. That would be my guess. They're trying a last-ditch effort to get you. Or maybe it's just revenge. Or some new faction that wants to take this planet. I don't know. And I don't care. The only thing I know is that I will put my body between you and anything that goes boom." His body vibrated, but he was solid against me. I believed he would try.

He'd lost his wife to a ship exploding in the war.

"You weren't with her." I'd give him the respect of acknowledging what we both knew he was talking about. "But you're here with me."

He kissed the top of my forehead. "And I'm not going anywhere. It's a good thing I came back to bed. Headache. Too much cream, I think, in the dessert. Otherwise I'd be running across The Farm to get to you right now."

I laughed at the ridiculousness of the fact that we were talking about cream before a thought dawned on me. "Waverly's place? It's so exposed."

"Yes, it is, and they knew that when they built it out there. I'm hoping it wasn't the target. Normally I don't want the guys' super senses, but right now I wouldn't mind it."

I swallowed. "Would it be on the tablet?"

He nodded. "Would be great if I had mine on me. But I'm not running back into the bedroom to grab it and leaving you here."

It had been quiet for a moment. Maybe he could... Another explosion shook the building. My ears rang, and I covered them, making myself as small as I could against him. I didn't know why I did it. Instinct. I wanted to be as tiny as I could be. And I should be brave, the kind to argue that I'd keep him safe and not the other way around, but the truth was that Trenton at least had a sense of what to do right now, and I really did not.

My ears continued to buzz, and I wondered if they'd ever stop.

He shouted over the noise. "Just stay where you are. We're okay. We're right where we need to be to stay okay."

I almost asked if he was lying, only I really didn't want to know.

BOMB AFTER BOMB. If we were winning, I certainly couldn't tell. No, we'd come to The Farm and brought hell with us. Or maybe not. Maybe we'd stepped right into it. This was my second time living in crisis with Trenton. He had my back, always. If I could hear over the noise, or believed I could make him hear me, I'd tell him that I would never be able to repay him. That I was grateful. That if this was the end, I was glad to be here with him.

The door swung open, and he lunged forward like he would attack with just his body anyone who was there.

"Hold up." Kellan nodded at Trenton. "Just me. Not safe in here. The structure is coming down. It's almost over, and we've got them where we want them, but damage is damage." He rushed into the bedroom instead of toward us and came out with some clothes. With a flick of his hand, he threw a shirt to Trenton and an entire outfit to me.

Trenton took his hand off the top of the table as Kellan put his there. "Get changed under here. Okay, sweetheart?"

"Where are we going to go that's safe?" Trenton threw on a pair of shoes that he grabbed from the bedroom and brought me a pair, too. I guessed Kellan hadn't thought of our feet. That was okay. I loved that he was here. Things were just better when we were all together, and if I couldn't have all of them with me, I was glad to see two of them at the same time in this crisis.

"Believe it or not, outside. They're aiming for the buildings. It would be worse, but the Dark Planets have shown up with reinforcements."

I blinked. Had I heard him right? "The Dark Planets?"

"That's right. They caught wind of the plan when these guys stole their frickin' ships. Came after them. Apparently, there is a lot of hostility toward Evander for taking what they wanted and for coming after you, Sienna."

Now I knew I had to have hit my head. "Why would they care about me?"

"You're a legend. Apparently." He took my hand and pulled me out from under the table.

"I'm a what?"

Trenton looked up at the ceiling and then rushed to the door, pulling it open. I followed him with Kellan behind me. He hadn't answered me, and that was okay since my ears were ringing again. Was this going to be permanent damage?

In a matter of minutes, we were outside in the open. This was safe? It would only take one bomb to take out all of us now.

"Hey." Diana rushed up next to me. "We were worried about you."

She had a toddler in her arms. I don't know why that struck me silent. But there she was, holding a baby in the middle of this mess. These women—Diana, Waverly, and even their friends who weren't here, Paloma and Amber— they were mothers. Melissa had raised children in this mess.

We hadn't had to face this where I was from. It was remote, difficult, but it hadn't until recently been violent.

Why hadn't I appreciated that gentle existence? I knew the answer. It was because of my role in all of it.

I found my voice. "Hi."

She put her hand on my arm. "I lose my voice in stress, too, sometimes."

"How do you do this? With kids?" I nodded toward them. Not that I had that happening in my future. I was probably not going to live that long. But the question remained just the same. How was she out here with a little one that she was responsible for?

"I can't help but be filled all the time with the optimism that things are going to be okay." My ears rang, but I could hear her just fine. "I hold on to that idea. If we wait to have our lives until everything is okay, then we're always going to be waiting. We have to act like there is an end to this, we have to believe there will be. And when needed, we have to be very careful to take care of those who need us." She visibly swallowed. "Don't get me wrong. I grew up hiding under floorboards on Mars Station when Sandler Cartel would attack. I didn't want this for my kids. But I wanted to have a family. I made it through, and they will too. The difference will be this will stop before the time they're older. I just know it."

She didn't know what we were going to do, how we planned to take on Evander. I made a decision as I stood watching the mess around us unfold. I would do whatever I had to do so that Evander didn't hurt these people anymore. She would get to have her future. Her kids would have that life.

Kellan grabbed my arm. "Look." He pointed upward. "See? Those aren't our ships. We're up there, too. But the one about to blow the shit out of that bastard firing at us? That's from some planet that the people here don't even know the name of. But they came to save us because of you."

There he was again with that. "What does that mean?"

Diana shook her head. "It means that you are a symbol to them. Even off your planet. They know who you are, and they're not happy that Evander took you."

How was that even possible? "I'm not some sort of icon. I was of small importance because of the weird things I can do on a planet on the edge of the universe."

"Yes." Kellan met my gaze. "Until your father went around telling the story of what happened. Now you're some kind of symbol of oppression they want to save."

My stomach clenched. My missing father. We had no idea what happened to him after he got me away from the Evander ship. He saved me, and he vanished.

"He's here?" I looked around. Why was I just hearing about this now? That should have been the first thing they told me. "Where?"

Kellan pointed. "Up there."

My father was on a ship up there? "I..."

Trenton sighed. "They don't have parents. They don't really get it. First I'm hearing of it, too, or I'd have told you earlier. Parents are important." He shoved at Kellan's shoulder.

The Super Soldier rolled his eyes. "Yes, that's why I'm telling her."

I took a long breath. The when of this really didn't matter under the circumstances. This was so strange. I was some kind of icon, the Dark Planets had risen up to save us, and my father was up there. My father who was absolutely not a man who knew how to conduct a war or even use ships that shot things.

I grabbed Diana's arm. "Is Waverly okay?"

"Oh yes, they're fine. They have a whole system that makes it hard to see their house from space, hard on the sensors. We can't seem to make that happen here. It has to do with how it was constructed. Her husbands had the good sense to make it that way. We built ours before that." She shook her head. "But it's okay. Because you and the Dark Planets have put an end to all of this."

Her words made me look down at my wrist. I was back to level nine. No, I wasn't quite done yet. I should probably not be out in public at all lest it rise again. But what was I supposed to do? The world was on fire around us, and I had to wait like everyone else.

Or did I? I held up my wrist. There were kids here. What if they were more susceptible to what I had than an adult? I looked at Trenton. "I'm at nine."

"I'd be shocked if you weren't. Stress raises your numbers. It lowers when you can relax. The few minutes you get to do that. Good food. Some rest. It goes down."

I supposed that was true, but it wasn't an exact science. I'd been okay on Artemis in the beginning, and still the numbers had risen. I didn't know if there was a one-to-one ratio. As if I'd conjured him because I needed answers, Wade appeared in the crowd, striding toward us.

"I knew Trenton would keep you safe." He pulled me to him in a strong hug. I closed my eyes for a second and breathed him in. He wasn't in his normal clothes but a white lab coat and a pair of scrubs beneath. He'd been working.

I pulled back. "Are you okay?"

"Yes. It's a mess. Lots of injured, but we stabilized and

got the machines going." He turned toward Diana. "Cash says he'll find you when this is over. Where is Devil?" He stared at Trenton and then Kellan. "I know there is something he wanted to do and now might be the completely right time to do it."

Kellan shook his head. "It's done."

It was? When had that happened? The problem with a secret plan that had to stay that way was that I got no updates. I had no idea what I was supposed to do to help, if anything, or how anything had progressed. It didn't matter. I wasn't going to find out before they wanted to tell me, like my father.

"Wade, my number is back to nine."

He nodded, not looking the least bit surprised. "Let's go put you on Artemis. Trenton, is she okay to sit on docked?"

"Yep," he nodded. "If the hangar is safe. Is it?"

"Safe enough. This is wrapping up." Kellan strode forward. "Besides, even with everything she's been through, Artemis could take the ceiling landing on her and not break. That ship is fucking amazing." He winced. "Sorry, Sienna."

"Yeah?" I grinned. "Fuck it. Fuck. Fuck-Fuck."

Kellan smirked at me. "Think you're funny?"

"I don't think it, I know it."

His smile broadened until he was outright grinning. He looked skyward. "The ships are all landing. Wade, they'll need you again. If you want to put her on Artemis in some medical capacity, I think you should go ahead and do that now."

"I'll stay with her," Trenton offered, "and work on Artemis while I'm there. Kellan, I'm sure there'll be things you have to do, too."

"Yep." He winked at me.

This was downright playful for Kellan. The thought

occurred to me that I could zap him right then. He'd asked for it more than once. Wanted to know how I did it. The truth was that I wanted to know how I did it, too. And the answers I needed were probably landing on a ship. My father had to know something. At the very least, maybe he'd heard rumors explaining why.

I needed to know why Evander wanted me so badly they'd gone to so much ridiculous trouble.

I wasn't a legend or an idol. I was just a woman. It was time I got answers.

I was tired of being a passive member of my own existence.

If I was ever going to keep up with all of these men, I had to do better.

Even if it was just with the time I had left.

* * *

I knew he would come. Even as I waited in the med bay of Artemis, I knew my father would find me. He'd come all this way, done a tremendous amount of work to try to keep me alive.

It had been years since we'd seen each other. But the last few minutes seemed to take years.

Trenton didn't say anything. He was good about being quiet, about not needing explanations of things when there weren't any to give. Life was tricky. It was messy. The man who had done all these things for me had been pretty much a stranger when we'd lived on our home planet.

Still, he was my father. What did that mean? How much did relationships that we didn't choose define us?

I really didn't know.

The sound of the door opening alerted me he was there.

Behind him, Anders stood. He nodded at me and then Trenton before vanishing back into the hall.

"Sir." Trenton acknowledged my father who never looked at him, his gaze solely on me.

Tears pooled in my eyes, but I didn't let them fall. I didn't want to remember these moments through the haze of crying. If I could manage it, I was going to figure out how to stay grounded in this present so I always remembered it.

"Dad," I managed to say. "You saved me."

Trenton quietly exited the room. On this broken ship, they weren't leaving me, just giving me the illusion of space. If he wanted to, Anders could hear and repeat all that was said.

"Sienna." He walked to me and stopped at the shield. I still read nine on my arm, but who knew what that meant. The way I worried about Diana's toddler, I was going to be concerned about him. He was older. I owed the people around me at least as much care as they gave me. Maybe more, considering all the things that were done and manipulated just to see to my well-being.

He took a long breath. "I was hoping they'd have fixed you. Are you okay?" He put his hand over the screen.

I sighed. "I think that depends on your definition of the word. In some ways, yes, I've never been better. In others, I'm living in a constant borderline state of upheaval that I don't know what to do about. And then there is the daily question of what my number will be on my wrist. That tells me how sick I am that day. It changes. Up and down. That determines a lot." I realized I might not be making a lot of sense. "I'm okay, Dad. They're trying to fix me."

We were going to cross the galaxy to try to fix me. Lie to some very good people to get that done. The thought bothered me more and more. All of these strangers who'd stepped up for me deserved better than us plowing open the black hole and risking everyone's safety. Even if in the process we were able to take down Evander.

Or maybe it was the right thing to do. It wasn't like I'd ever had a huge amount of parental lessons in morality and ethical behavior from the man who stood in front of me.

Sometimes it really sucked being able to see things from all sides of an issue.

"They took you, and I couldn't let them have you. I had to try to do something. Your mother... she's in Sandler space, hidden, so that they can't use her against you. Not that they can do that anymore. All of Evander seems to be stopped."

I touched the glass between us as though some of my warmth might penetrate into him. He'd had a hard time. It must have been lonely and miserable. "Thank you, Dad."

"I... I feel like we let you down." He looked at his feet and then back up at me. "You were so special, so talented. Tradition dictated we give you to the temple for a destiny that was bigger than working in a shop with us. But truthfully, my love, it never sat right with us. Were you very unhappy?"

I blinked, my good intentions of not crying fleeing. Okay. I was going to cry, and there wasn't a thing I was able to do about it. I wiped them away but more came. "No, Dad. I wasn't happy. I'm not made for what I had to do. The truth is that despite all the circumstances that I keep finding myself in, I am just a woman who would have done very well with a simple life. Even if I never used my abilities at all. I don't really understand why I have them. Human beings can't do what I do. What any of us could do. It's not normal."

He nodded, and his throat muscles constricted as he visibly swallowed. "That's what I thought. About your happiness, not about your abilities. Surely they explained that to you?"

I pushed through the haze. He had said something very important. "Who would have explained what to me?"

"The people who ran the temple. They were supposed to explain."

I'd still been considered a novice when my uncle turned me over to Evander. If something was going to be explained, it had not yet been done. "No one told me anything."

"Listen, I'm not a scientist. You must have seen from being out here that people are a lot more educated than we were in other parts of the universe."

I tapped on the glass. "Dad, you somehow managed to inspire groups of people to fight for some idea of me. I think you have proven to be very smart if not formally educated. On our planet, you weren't a dummy. Give yourself a break. You need to tell me how you did that, by the way."

He smiled, his first real one since he'd come in the room. "I had a lot of help from some people who first rescued me from Evander. They used to be pirates. One of them has a famous last name, Sandler. Anyway, they helped. They're very persuasive, and one of them, Bo, he's from our planet originally. Worked in the mining division, so to him you really were some kind of important figure. It wasn't all on me."

Were there Sandlers everywhere? That was a question for another time. "Go on, Dad. Tell me why I can do these things."

"The women on our planet, when they've been studied by smarter people than me, they are shown to have—I might get these words wrong—lower levels of activity in their brains in some parts. I think it's called the left hippocampus."

It was like he was speaking gobbledygook to me. I had no idea what in the universe he meant by that. The door opened and closed. This time it was Kellan who stepped in. He didn't say a word but approached fast.

"Keep speaking." He addressed my father. "This is interesting."

I smirked. "They can hear and see and just generally do anything a lot better than we can. There really isn't privacy with Super Soldiers around. You get used to it."

My dad looked between us. "Is he your... boyfriend? I thought maybe the one who walked me in was but then you were in here with the one with the long hair and..." Realization swept over my father's face fast. "All of them. Like the former pirates who helped me. You have one of those multiple relationships going on. So unusual where we are from, and so common here. Seems everyone I run into has one of those. The people who own this place, they're in a plural sort of relationship."

I didn't know the first thing about how Diana's multiple marriage worked outside of the fact that it did. He wasn't wrong. Love was love here, and it came in many forms.

"That's right. I am with more than one man." I smiled. "Seven of them, actually."

He paled. "Seven? Are you constantly exhausted?"

"Dad," I practically shouted. "I'm not... getting into that with you. Please go on. Kellan might actually understand what you're saying to me. The left... what was it?"

Kellan pulled over a chair and motioned for my father to sit in it while he answered me instead of my father. "Hippocampus. He means the limbic system. It's where the subcortical structures meet the cerebral cortex. Thought to be responsible for motivation, learning, memory, that kind of thing. Go on. Lower level of activity. That's interesting.

So she lowers the use of her left hippocampus to take on other people's shit." He winced. "Sorry, I curse. A lot. I didn't have parents. They made me in a lab, so I have no idea how to talk to you."

My father stared at Kellan for a long moment. "I like you."

I might never understand male relationships. Not even if I lived to be three hundred years old. "Please. Can we continue?"

"You also decrease activity in your superior temporal gyrus."

Kellan sighed. "Language. Sounds." He answered my unasked question as to what that did. "Anything else?"

"The front lobe—I think that's what it's called—it also showed less activity. I've never really understood any of that."

My Super Soldier rocked back on his feet. "A whole shit ton of stuff gets controlled in the frontal lobe. So what you're saying is that when she does these things, the zapping, the emotion, she is actually using less of her brain power than when she's not. Like she's simply controlling her mind differently." By the end, he was downright jumpy for Kellan. "That is so interesting. And so... perfect."

I wasn't following him at all. My father finally sat down. We both openly stared at Kellan. "Why is it perfect?" My dad finally asked him.

"Because Super Soldiers. We use our brains differently, too. That's what we do. Like when I want to listen a great distance away—say when I can't sleep and I have to find your heartbeat to make it through the night—I unconsciously ask my brain, my frontal lobe as it is, to work a little harder. I don't do it with thought. I just do it. That's what you're doing. To take on emotion, to focus that so hard at someone that you literally zap their brain, you cool yours down. Sienna, it's such good news."

I put my head against the glass. "Kellan, I'm still not following you."

"Not everyone can mess with their brain like that. It's a genetic ability. Like... rolling your tongue." He pushed his out, showing me he could do that. I picked my head off the glass so that I could show him the same. Yes, I could do that, too. "The women in your family. Natural selection—that's an old phrase—you ladies are genetically predetermined to be able to do that with your brain. You can roll your brain."

The door opened and closed. "Are you saying to her what I think you are?" Anders walked fast.

"I am." Kellan outright grinned at Anders. "We can fix her. We can get rid of what is making her sick."

Now they really had my attention. "How?"

"We can make you like us. You could do it. We can make you one of us."

It took me a long moment to understand what he meant. "A Super Soldier?"

"Well, not full on. I mean, why would you need to be able to shoot better or target people? You don't need to do that. But there are reasons Evander picked the people they picked to make us from. They adapted genetic ability. We can do that to you because you already have the key point that makes us, well, us. You are capable of brain adaptivity. You can handle some of what we are." He smiled. "We can take some of the technology we have that helps us be us, and we can use that on you. Sienna, you could actually survive it. We don't need Evander. Fuck them and all that noise. We can fix you. You could be like us."

I sat down on the bed. Was what he said possible?

"IS THAT SOMETHING THAT YOU WANT?" Anders met my gaze through the glass. "If we could do it, would you want that?"

It was hard to speak. "I... I don't want to be sick if I don't have to be. I don't want people getting hurt. I don't like lying." He would know what that meant. "Or being a risk to people."

He nodded fast. "I don't think Kellan is off the mark here. There are things to consider. I mean, you'd have to go through a cellular change. That can't be an easy thing to do. They grew us in a petri dish and then changed us as babies. Plus, I'm not sure this is legal here."

Kellan threw over a table, and the whole room went silent. Anders adjusted his stance slightly. Was he preparing to have to fight Kellan? Anxiety made me stand up straighter.

"Something wrong?" Anders lowered his voice.

"I don't give a shit about the legality of this. Surely there must be a way to handle it. Considering the extenuating circumstances of what happened to her. I'm not suggesting that we go around altering the general population to take care of their aches and pains. What happened to her happened because of people like us. I mean, Devil was actually there. We have to fix it. Period. She's ours. Don't give me reasons why it won't work."

Anders held up his hands as though he was in surrender. "I want to do it, too. But take it down a notch before her father absconds with her again and we never see her for the rest of our lives. We know he can do it. He's done it before."

My father rose slowly. "What I see is a lot of emotion because you love my daughter. Maybe you don't know how to control those feelings. It's hard for some young people to work that out. I'm not concerned for her safety with you. Just the opposite. She said she wants it. If you need me to run her off to some place we can do this without the law being a problem, we can do that, too."

"No one is running anywhere," Blaze strode through the door. "We can do this here. As far as I know, the laws on The Farm don't prohibit this. We might have more of a problem on Mars Station."

I motioned toward Blaze. "Dad, I'm sorry. We didn't do introductions. This is Blaze. He's in charge of this group. Anders. And Kellan."

My father rapidly blinked. "This is all going to take some getting used to. When this is over, will you come home?"

I hadn't even thought about it before he asked. I didn't know what I'd do when this was over. Not really. I hadn't given much thought to the idea of next because I hadn't considered that I might have that. Still, I could answer him. "Not home. That's gone. We all went there. It's pretty decimated. I don't think my future is there. Having said that, I need to know what kind of plans these guys would like to have. Unless they tell me otherwise, I'm with them."

Kellan's shoulders seemed to visibly untighten. "Where you go, I go."

"Who is going to do this cellular change?" My dad seemed to have quickly moved on. "You three?"

"No." Blaze shook his head. "Wade. With some help probably from some other doctors. There are good ones here. But it'll be Wade."

He was going to hate this. I didn't have to alter my brain waves or whatever I was doing to understand that. Wade was going to have a big fucking problem with this.

* * *

"So we're completely shifting gears?" Wade ran a hand through his hair. "Everything we discussed is just not happening?"

We'd definitely gotten attention about this process. Within minutes of the conversation, Wade and Trenton had arrived with Corbin and Devil. The latter two had told the former what they had in mind. Trenton was surprisingly quiet on the subject but Wade, as predicted, was not. My father had left, going to find some place to sleep for the night and something to eat. He didn't need to be here for this discussion, and I was fairly certain that he found the guys as a group pretty overwhelming. That made sense. They were absolutely a lot to take all at once if you weren't used to them.

Blaze held a finger to his mouth, reminding Wade about the subjects we weren't discussing. The doctor threw his head back and laughed. "Really? You're serious? I think we're maybe past the point of that at the moment."

"You want this?" Trenton asked me.

I smiled at him. He'd have no way of knowing that I'd already been asked. "If it can work."

"Sienna." Wade looked pale. "We don't know any of the long-term results of this. Okay. If we can make the science work. If I can get nanos from Canyon's eye device that Ari dismantled... and reprogram them to work on you at a cellular level, to change you, then yes, we can probably make your immune system fight off what is in you like a Super Soldier. But we have no idea what else could happen. These guys have had their whole lives to learn to tune out sounds they don't want to hear, to control themselves so they don't hurt people. I... I'm not even sure what to antici-pate because nothing like this has ever been done before."

I raised my hand. "I'm willing to volunteer."

"Could it kill her?" Corbin crossed his arms over his chest.

Wade hung his head. "There is always the possibility of death. In every surgery."

"She could die right now from what's happening to her, and it won't be pretty." Devil spoke from the corner. He met my gaze and gave me a small smile. "It won't be pleasant. She'll go through hell, and there won't be a thing Wade can do to stop it. She's already at a nine. Let's not push her body into level ten when we can't be near her before we give this a try. Blaze and I can teach her to ignore excessive sounds the same way we do with the juveniles when they come out of the nursery seclusion back at Evander headquarters. I don't know if we're voting. It's her body. She told us what she wanted."

Corbin tilted his head. "I only asked a question. I didn't

offer an opinion. The only one objecting to this is the person who has to actually make this happen. Can you do it, Wade? Or is this whole conversation for naught because you aren't capable of it?"

Wade straightened his shoulders and advanced on the much bigger man. "I'm fucking capable of it."

"Okay," Blaze spoke loudly, and they all shut up. "What do you need?"

"It's not the kind of thing one attempts alone if one doesn't have to." He'd officially taken to speaking in third person. I didn't know if that was a good thing or a bad thing. I'd never seen Wade do that before. "I need Cash, Lewis, Ari, and Waverly. I'd love to have Amber and Dane, but if that isn't possible, and it probably isn't, then those five are who I need. So if Sterling and Canyon or Rohan could send those folks over in the morning, that would be great."

The guys started to grin. It took me a second to catch on to the reasons for their smiles. Wade had just addressed the Super Soldiers not here as though he'd been certain they were listening.

"Think about it tonight, my love." He walked to the glass partition and leaned against it. "You can change your mind in the morning. We have a lot of the tools we need already. Yeah... I know." He put his finger to his mouth, reminding me we couldn't talk about this.

There were so many unknowns. I wanted a meal and a shower. Now that the adrenaline of everything had worn off, I was spent. I looked at my number. It stayed at nine. That was good because I was achy and sore on top of everything else. My chest felt tight. Was that nerves or the virus?

"I'm not one hundred percent." I had to be honest with Wade. He couldn't do his job if I weren't up-front. I wanted him to love on me, to be just my guy, but the truth was he was also my doctor. I had to let him play both roles.

He sank to the ground on the outside of the glass, so I did the same on my end. We could be face-to-face that way. His smile held no mirth to it. "Symptoms?"

"I'm achy. Sore. Just not myself."

"Okay. Could one of you get her some food? Sienna, I'm going to let you out to bathe and relax. You can go back to your room on this ship and use the bathroom."

A thought dawned on me. "It's cool and comfortable on here. The last time I flew on Artemis, it had no air-cooling ability."

"While we were eating dinner, the crews started working on her. Most of these guys trained with Tommy Sandler when he was here. They're very proficient at fixing up fast. Kind of like triage for the ship." Trenton smiled. He headed toward the door. "I'll get the food. It's way past breakfast. Almost lunch."

Blaze nodded. "Everyone should eat and sleep if they can. If she's doing this tomorrow, we all need to be on for her and not tired. Wade, you have to force yourself to get some rest. Can you do that?"

With a salute, Wade rose and walked over to the door to let me out of the separated room. "I will. I have to talk to Canyon and Ari first. This will be a no go if I can't use the nanos."

"We'd know by now if you couldn't." Devil headed toward the exit. "I promise you that."

It was a strange world where there were whole portions of conversations happening that I could never hear or know about because they were out of my range. Although I supposed that might change. Tomorrow.

This all happened very fast. The decision was made

and thus it was happening. Just that fast. I could change my mind, but at least at the moment as I walked toward the shower, I was at peace with this. Whatever happened, there couldn't be lasting consequences for the whole galaxy because they decided to save me.

Or at least I couldn't think of any.

Everything spun so fast all of the time, I'm not sure I could know what was about to happen until it actually did.

"Did your father ever say how he knew?" Wade called out to me as I walked toward the bathroom. "How he knew what your brain can do?"

That was a good question. "He said the people who ran the temple were eventually going to tell me. Some kind of tests that had once been done."

Wade nodded slowly. "I bet whoever tested all the women, they're why Evander was out there looking to begin with. Those tests are why they found your uncle to start. It was too remote for Evander to spend that much time seeking gossipy leads about women with powers. They already knew."

That made sense, too. The pieces were falling together. The only question was could we do what the guys wanted to do in order to fix me?

* * *

My shower had been wonderful, and I came out to find an egg dish that was filling and also tasty. I was still achy, and my numbers hadn't gone down just because of a warm shower and a full belly.

The guys were gone except for Trenton who was asleep on the small bed where I imagined I was supposed to spend the night. He snored lightly, his head turned to the side as he lay on his back. Trenton's long hair was across my pillow.

I sighed. Like Kellan the last time, I should kick Trenton out of my bed. But I wasn't going to. I was so screwed up on timing. Should I be sleeping right now? Running around? Doing push-ups? I smiled at that thought. I'd never done any that I could remember.

With nothing pressing, I crawled in next to him. He stirred, lifting his head. "Did you eat?"

"I did, thanks. You look spent."

Trenton snuggled against me, drawing me closer so that he held me from behind. "You smell so good."

"Thanks." He did too.

"Artemis, turn off the lights in this room." They dimmed immediately, and despite the fact that it was daytime, the room was immediately cloaked in darkness. It was soothing, and he drew me even closer.

"Trenton," I whispered in case he'd fallen back asleep already.

He lifted his head. "You okay? Scared about tomorrow?"

"I'm not actually. I should be, but I'm too spent, too tired of being sick. What I wanted to say to you is that you've twice now taken care of me when I could have been killed. The planet. Last night under the table. Thank you. For being there each time. Thank you."

He smoothed his finger over my bottom lip. "I think I knew even when you were in the cryogenic chamber that I was going to love you. I shouldn't. You deserve someone less destroyed than me. But I knew that I would. You saved me, Sienna. You are a miracle to me. I will always be there to keep you safe. Of that, I promise."

There was no way he could make such an oath to me,

and yet I believed him. The more I knew Trenton, the more I understood he never said or did anything he didn't believe he could go through with. He intended to be there for me every second he could be.

I pushed his hair out of his eyes. "I didn't save you. Just the opposite. You keep saving me. And when you needed me on that little ship where we got caught, I had to leave you there. Plus, you then turned around and saved us all again."

He snorted. "I made the lights flash. You took down a ship full of people."

"Which I could only do because—"

His mouth touched mine, the gentlest of kisses. "We saved each other that day. How about we go with that?"

I touched the side of his face. "Okay."

"Besides, what I meant was that you saved me on the inside. I've only been living for revenge for so long. I forgot how it was to feel like this, to be alive. Inside and out."

There was no question that Trenton had loved his late wife. I didn't feel any jealousy toward her or even the slightest bit of angst that he had loved someone before me. If anything, I was grateful for her. Someone had taught this man how to care, and it hadn't been his family. At least from what he'd told me the night on the planet in the rain.

He traveled his hand over my side. "Should I leave you alone to sleep?"

It was more like the opposite problem. "I'm the one who woke you."

His mouth met mine again, and this time I kissed him back. His lips were soft, and he sighed against me as our lips caressed.

He pulled back just a little bit and stroked his finger down the side of my face. "I'd do this differently if I could."

Tilting my head, I could only make out the outline of his strong features in the dark. "What do you mean?"

"Flowers. Roses. Wooing you. That's how this is done with women in this day and age. You should be making us work for this. All of us. We plowed into your life. You want this with us, right? Not just because it happens to be happening?"

I sat up on my elbow. "There's nothing I want more than what we're building. That's why I want to live to see it through. I want whatever comes next."

He stroked his hand down the front of my clothes, lifting the shirt up to expose my skin underneath. His hand caressed the place over my stomach where I curved a little bit. "We get you healthy and we figure out where to go to make a life. Maybe it's here. Maybe it's somewhere else. And we get busy loving each other for the rest of our days." He rolled me over so that I was on top of him. "Not every day will be perfect, but they'll be ours."

I kissed his neck, and his hips jerked beneath me. We were both dressed, and I knew enough now to understand what an impediment that was to what I wanted to do with Trenton. If it was all going to change tomorrow, I wanted tonight with Trenton to be hot and messy.

He drew my head down until we could kiss. Again and again. Although I was on top of him, there was no question about which one of us was in charge. Trenton was leading me through this, and I was happy to follow. He tugged at my shirt, and I finally helped him by throwing it off. I'd find it later.

He caressed my breasts, squeezing them with both hands at the same time. "I've dreamed of these. I wake up hard and aching. Nothing takes care of the pain. My fist and my hand just aren't what I needed."

My breath increased. I was practically panting, and we'd hardly started yet. "What is it that you need?"

"I need to be buried inside of you, feel your warm, soft pussy all around me. I need to feel your body take pleasure from mine. I need to know that I gave it to you."

I leaned down to kiss him on his chin. "Then take what you want from me because, sweetheart, I want it, too."

He laughed. "You just gave me a nickname. That one belongs to me."

Trenton flipped me over, flattening himself against me so that my breasts were pressed up against his chest. He still had his shirt on. That was so unfair. "Why are you dressed and I'm only half that way?"

Without a word, he stripped himself of his top so that we were skin-to-skin. He pushed against me again, sighing when my hardened nipples caressed his skin. Jolts of pleasure shot through me. Yes, I wanted this. So much.

We stripped each other of the rest of our clothes. It was good to be close to him like this, right to bathe myself in his scent, to know that I would smell him on me for the rest of the day. There was something so primal about that, so correct to be joined as tightly as one human can be to another. That was what I wanted with Trenton.

He kissed me again. This time, fully naked with his cock right where I could grind against him, it was so much more intimate. Tongues. Teeth. Trenton. Yes, fuck. I wanted more. I might have mumbled that against his mouth or maybe he read my mind.

Flipped over, I was finally beneath him. He ground against me, and a surge of pleasure moved through me. I cried out, hoping the world could hear how much that single movement made me feel fantastic. I giggled at the thought. I'd become a little bit of an exhibitionist. Or maybe it was Trenton making me this way.

I grasped his hard cock, making him cry out as I had. Sex with Trenton was so much fun. It was serious but also somehow joyful. Had I never understood before it could be both?

He scooted down my body, making it impossible to keep my hold on him, and placed his mouth right on my pussy. This time I didn't cry out. No, it was like I retreated into myself just to feel what he was doing, just to live in that one moment as his sweet tongue found my clit. He swirled his tongue over it again and again. Trenton seemed to understand I needed constant, consistent movement so my brain could anticipate what was coming and not have to wonder what was next. I ground against his mouth, taking what I needed, directing him until he had it perfectly just from following the cues of my body.

The buildup was huge. My body tensed again and again, as though it was holding on to everything he was giving me and didn't want to let it go. Finally, on a rush like I'd never known before, I exploded. It was like a detonation of pleasure, like a bomb going off in my body. Trenton pulled his mouth off of me, watching as I cried out, my body a spasm of movement I couldn't have controlled if I wanted to.

Seconds later, he was kissing me. He pulled his lips from mine only to speak words whispered into my ear. "I want to taste your pleasure. I want to capture it and never let it go."

With those words, he pushed inside of me. I hadn't come down yet, and the feel of his cock in me only spurred me back into the cycle his mouth had started. Trenton moved fast, bringing me to the precipice and not letting me down again. Over and over. It was like a spin of my senses. I held on for the ride and tried not to think because it was easier just to feel.

And how lovely to just get to do that.

It didn't take very long. We were both where we needed to be fast. Still, I hung on and so did he because when this was over, there would be no going back for either of us. This was our moment. This was the first time we were together.

This was how I could show him that I'd risk everything to keep us together.

Trenton's orgasm triggered another one in me.

It was perfection.

* * *

Trenton slept heavily, snoring lightly in my ear. I dozed, not really wanting to sleep through the day but loving how it felt to be tight against him and how good it was to be with him while he took rest he so obviously needed. I stroked my hand over the hard muscles on his back. He didn't stir. Eventually, the sound of his breathing next to me lulled me under. What did it matter what time it was? Day or night, people attacked us. We had to sleep when we could and not on some schedule that just didn't seem to fit in the constant state of chaos in which we existed.

I dreamed that I walked through a long field. I was barefoot, and the sunlight hit me like a warm bath of happiness.

Turning around, the dream changed, the sun fading. In its place were hundreds of thousands of Super Soldiers. I couldn't see their faces, but they were lined up and spoke in one voice.

"We're just across the black hole. We'll find a way to

you and all the others. Take back what is yours. You can never stop us, and your journey was for nothing."

I cried out, trying to run, but my bare feet were fused to the ground below me.

Still, in the distance, I saw a woman. It took me a moment to realize that it was me. I walked toward myself. She stopped in front of me. "You can stop them, Sienna. They don't get to win."

THE GUYS CAME and went during the night, which made me happy I'd slept most of the day. They each had things to do, and they weren't alone in their comings and goings. Everyone who knew what was happening seemed to be very agog about the whole thing.

Waverly took my temperature not short of three times, while every Super Soldier on the base stared at a computer screen where Cash and Wade were rewriting nanoprobes that had once been inside Canyon. I guessed they were going to be in me now.

There really wasn't much for me to do except sit still and wait for things to happen. It was also noisy as anything. Construction on Artemis had picked up speed. Someone—I suspected Trenton since he hadn't come back after he left to shower—was fixing the ship.

"Are we doing it here?" I cleared my throat to get everyone's attention. "On Artemis? Or are we doing it out there on the planet?"

Wade turned to meet my gaze. Worry lines had formed around his eyes. For his sake, as well as my own, I hoped this went well. He might never forgive himself if it didn't. I looked down at my number. Holding steady at nine. I supposed it was too much to ask of the universe to make it suddenly number three. And then magically to just be better and never sick again.

But that wasn't going to happen. I was going to have to have the procedure. I preferred that word to cellular organization, which was what Lewis kept calling it when he spoke. I shivered at the thought of that. No. I wasn't a medical person.

"Here." Wade smiled. "Artemis has been the site of some pretty amazing medical procedures before. I've been hearing about all of them. I've decided she's good luck."

I liked Artemis for many reasons. She might be the only ship I'd ever feel comfortable on. I mean, we crash-landed her and she was still not totally destroyed. That was the thing about her—she seemed to be able to take a lot of hits and still come out the other side.

"Do we need to be in space for the magic of Artemis to work?"

Wade pressed his hand on the glass. "No, we just need you to be here. You're the magic."

"Aww, good line." Cash threw a cup at him. "I never come up with any good lines. Diana must think I'm clueless most of the time when it comes to romance."

"I don't think that's how she feels." Sterling didn't look up from his tablet. "I can't believe we're doing this. I mean... are we really going to put the things that nearly utterly destroyed our lives into your girlfriend?"

Wade shot Sterling a look. "It wasn't the nanos that were the problem. It was what they had you do with them. Nanos didn't make you a killer. You were just forced to kill and happened to have them in you, making you really good at it. I just want the immune function. That's all."

The screen next to me flickered to life, and Amber Chen appeared in front of me. I blinked. What was she doing? "Hi."

Wade waved at her. "Amber. Good to have you sort of here."

"Yep. I couldn't believe the message I got. What you're doing is pseudo illegal on Earth." She looked over her shoulder. "It's sort of a gray area. I mean, you're not trying to make her a Soldier, so it's medical. I... I'm not sure what to say. I'm not sure I can help."

I stared at the beautiful woman who had invented the device that Wade used to save my life. "If it means anything, I want to try this. We have to do something." And if it didn't work, we were going to blow open the black hole. I couldn't imagine that wasn't illegal, and there was nothing pseudo about it.

"It does." She smiled. "I'm on my way to you. It won't matter in time. But I'm good with recovery, and my husbands need to check out some of the ships Sterling is building for us. Get them moved to Earth. Plus, Hunter has this whole thing with the water supply. We'll be there in five days."

One way or another, the next time I saw Amber, this would be done. A memory. Something I could remember doing and not something I had to get through. That was a nice thought. "Well, maybe we could have another meal or something."

She smiled. "I'd love that. I mean, I'll have the girls with me and every member of the Z Warriors'll probably follow me around but, yes, we can have a meal. I wasn't sure you'd want to after last time. I don't think we made the greatest impression, and then Devil absconded with you, so... Yes, I'd love to have lunch. Or something. Maybe drinks. Do you have drinks?"

I blinked. "I've never had a drink of alcohol."

Wade knocked on the glass. "We can amend that. Not tonight. But, yes, as soon as you're healthy. Alcohol would be fine.

Amber shook her head. "It's probably fine now, Wade. It's not like it's going to knock around with her numbers. They're already not good."

"Not the night before surgery, Dr. Chen." Wade's face hardened. "And I brought you on to assist, not contradict."

She whistled. "He really must love you, Sienna. It takes a lot to get Wade that touchy."

He waved his hand. "Ignore her. She's being obnoxious. We went through hell together. She knows full well that I'm always touchy."

Amber groaned. "See you guys in a few days. You'll do great, and then you'll have to let us know if you have any homicidal tendencies that make you emotionally blackmail someone into potentially getting themselves into trouble."

She turned off the screen, and I scratched my head. "I'm missing something."

"Blaze." Anders nodded toward him. "He guilted her into outing herself to her husbands who she was hiding from. It wasn't pretty. But he does know how to get people to do what he wants."

I loved this banter. I could listen to all of them talk all day and night. I'd rather not have to do it from behind this glass. That was another thing to look forward to.

"Will it hurt?" I hadn't asked, and it seemed like something I know.

Wade winced. "I think it probably will, but I will do

everything to make sure I do my best to mitigate that." He sighed. "I wish I could say no. We could maybe make it so you don't remember the pain."

I leaned back on the bed. "Use your best judgment."

Corbin opened the door and came inside with me. I stared at him, shaking my head. This was a constant problem. Wade didn't want them in here, and they didn't care. They were going to argue about it, and it was going to stress Wade out. He had not been the least bit amused to find Trenton with me. That was even scarier for him than the Super Soldiers, as Trenton could actually get really sick from me easier than these guys.

I pointed back at the door. "You should probably not make him upset right now."

"I'm not leaving you alone in the hours leading up to your surgery." He kissed my cheek. "Besides, Wade likes yelling at us. It's a good stress relief."

I put my head on Corbin's shoulder as he sat down. I didn't mind the company. It was nice to know that I wasn't going to be alone. Especially in these times when minutes felt like hours.

* * *

It was funny how things could be a hurry up and wait situation followed by so much immediate action it made my head spin. Or maybe it wasn't funny. Maybe that was just the sort of thing that was amusing to me.

But despite the fact that the minutes crawled in preparation and I had to get in and out of the med machine five times to check levels, whatever that meant, I was suddenly on the table with Waverly, Wade, Cash, Lewis, and Ari all around me. The last smiled down at me kindly.

"He's not wrong. Artemis has been good luck for all of us. We're going to take good care of you, and you won't remember this when it's over. You'll be out cold for most of it."

I nodded, but I had to add a caveat. "If I end up in cryo, it can't be more than a year."

"There's no reason we should have to put you in cryo." Cash looked at Wade. "Do you have plans for that?"

Wade shook his head. "None at all. But I do understand, my love. I know what you want. No waking up having lost too much time. I promise."

"You guys couldn't wait for me?" All heads turned as Melissa's husband Dane entered fast. "I rush from Mars Station to see this historic, albeit legally questionable, thing you guys are throwing yourself into, and you can't even wait for me to get here?"

Wade smiled, and so I took a deep breath. He was obviously glad to see Dane.

Waverly squeezed my hand before she put a device under my nose. "This is just oxygen."

* * *

"Sienna?" Wade's voice called out to me and drew me from the nothingness where I'd been. It was hard to think, like I was being asked to do so from inside some kind of fog. "Can you hear me?"

This was strikingly familiar. "I can."

"Good." He smoothed my hair again. Wade could be so gentle when he wasn't obsessing over things.

"If I open my eyes, are you going to be ten years older?"

He laughed, an easy sound. "Twenty, I'm afraid."

"What?" I tried to sit up but was quickly stopped by strong hands on my shoulders.

"Sorry. Bad joke. No, I'm only a few hours older. About eight of them. Rest. Don't dart up, although I'm impressed you could do that. Open your eyes for me so I can shine a light in them."

I groaned. "Not giving me a lot of incentive to actually open my eyes."

"I know. And if you could remember how unhappy you were during the procedure, you'd not want to do what I asked now either. But the good news is that we induced amnesia and you should have no idea. So please? Open your eyes?"

I did as he asked. He stared down at me for a second before he nodded like he could tell I could see him. Then he shined the light in my eyes. I took that for two seconds before I swatted at his hand. "That hurts. Stop."

He pulled the light away. "Welcome back, my love."

I really loved the way he called me *my love*. I smiled at him. "How did I do?"

"Good. It seems to be working." He held up my arm so I could see. My number was down to one. I stared at it like I couldn't believe it. It was at one?

He smoothed my forehead again. "I expect it to be zero in a minute. If it stays that way for several days, I can take the device out of your arm. You'll be cleared."

I swallowed. That was the best possible news. I couldn't control myself and threw my arms around him. He held on tight. "I think it's working in many ways. You should be weak and exhausted. But you've twice managed to get up now when you should be flat on your back. We tried to contain the nanos to your immune system, but they tend to do what they do. We'll have to watch it."

Right then, I didn't care. Not at all. "You saved me."

"Not quite yet." He shook his head. "Almost. And it wasn't me. It was Kellan's idea. I almost said I wouldn't do it because I was too nervous about what could happen to you. I need to do some testing on you. For just a second."

I heard the telltale whoosh of the door opening as Blaze strode in. "Her heartbeat is the same. I can hear it. Nothing changed."

Wade nodded once. "Okay."

"Can you hear my heartbeat?" Blaze asked me, and Wade rolled his eyes. Maybe he didn't want to do it this way?

I listened but no, I couldn't hear anything. "Nothing."

Blaze nodded once. "You did it." He must have been speaking to Wade, because I hadn't done anything that I could remember. I'd been a passive participant in this. I looked up and then caught my breath.

What the heck was that? It was like balls of light were floating and banging into each other with little people singing in the center. I couldn't hear what they were saying, but they were definitely singing. How did I know that?

"Something's wrong." I grabbed Wade's hand. "I'm seeing things."

"Oh." He laughed. "Don't worry on that. The little men singing are always there. Sorry you didn't notice it before."

I stared at him, my mouth falling open. This wasn't real. In a million years that would not have been the answer Wade would give to me. I backed up on the bed. "What's going on here?"

Blaze waved his hand. "It's just a little singing. Why make a big deal about it?"

I pressed my head against my knee. I wasn't awake. This was some kind of dream. Or hallucination. Or something.

"I'm not awake. This isn't real."

"That's a shame." Wade sighed. "It would have been nice, wouldn't it, to have been done so easy? All fixed. Not sick anymore. No pain. You can't remember what happened to you. All better. Boom. Time for your happy ending."

I made myself stare at the not-Wade. "Neither Wade nor I are the type to particularly believe in happy endings. We're too real for that."

"That's a shame." Blaze sighed. "Singing men in rainbows or whatever seems like a nice existence. Guess we'll see you soon."

Pain assaulted my senses, and I screamed, the operating room in Artemis coming into view. Sweat was all over my body, and I flailed against the restraints that held me down.

"She's up. Again." Dane shook his head, a sympathetic look in his eyes. "It's so hard to keep them under with the nanos."

Wade squeezed my hand but wasn't looking at me, his gaze upward on the machine. "Yes, but it's working. I'm sorry. This is hard, my love." He leaned over and kissed me. "But the machines we put in you, the nanos, they are actually making you better."

I screamed again. There was pain everywhere. I hadn't known that anything could hurt this much. Every joint, every muscle, aches and waves of agony rode through me like it was going to drag me under and never let me go.

"We have to give her something." Ari stepped away from the table. "I can drug Super Soldiers. I can drug her. She has less of what makes them, them."

Wade slammed his hand on the table. "I don't want her to hurt. I want it less than anyone alive. But it's working. If you give that to her now and screw it up, this whole thing will have been for nothing." He took a visible breath. "Can you hold on, my love? Can you?"

Waverly squeezed my hand. "She can. I know you can. Because you're strong and everyone here is doing this with you. I know only you have to endure it, but The Farm is all holding their breath and waiting for you to get through this. There are Super Soldiers pacing in the hall in terror—and they've taken on the universe in battle. You can do this. I know you can."

Her words helped. I drifted away, back to that place with the dancing unicorns. Or whatever it was. Singing something or other. And then there was just nothing.

* * *

The next time I woke up, it was on a medical bed with machines beeping everywhere. Yep, that seemed real to me. Wade's back was to me as he looked at a machine. The room was filled with the doctors and Waverly in the corner talking to Amber on a screen in a low voice. I couldn't hear what they said.

My love turned around. "Hey, how are you doing? We just gave you something for the pain. It should help." He wasn't doing that lovey gooey thing he did in my dream where he pushed my bangs off my forehead. I wanted that. But my throat hurt, and I wasn't sure if it was worth it to ask for it.

"Pain?" He winced. "I'm sorry. I was worried about the meds screwing up the nanos, but I think we have that sorted. So you should start to feel better soon."

Finally, I found my voice. "I had a dream about you smoothing the hair off my forehead."

He blinked. "Oh... I..."

Dane strode over. "I think that sounds like a good idea, Doctor. You're relieved of duty, so to speak. Good work. If this happens, it's because of what you did in there. But now you need to be her guy and not her doctor. So sit down and smooth her hair off her face. Women like that."

Wade moved fast. He grabbed a chair and pulled it over before he sat in it and started to do just what I asked of him.

"There were singing men in bubbles. Or something."

He nodded. "Very screwed up things happened in your mind, I imagine. I can't tell you what it means to me to be here with you right now. That your eyes are open and you're here with me."

I stared at his face. It was good to be here, too. I hoped. "It worked?"

"We'll know soon."

Yes, this wasn't that fake world where everything was just fine. That had never been my reality and never would be.

* * *

I must have slept on and off. I didn't feel pain, it was like there was nothing at all. When I opened my eyes, Wade was there. I never saw the others. They must have been kept away because someone had convinced them it was truly a good idea. I knew for a fact they weren't great at obeying rules when it didn't suit them.

The room was quiet. Only Dane stood in the corner, watching machines and tapping on his tablet. He smiled at something and tapped again. Wade snored gently, his head at a strange angle, his face not restful in sleep. I hated to think of him not being comfortable.

Dane met my gaze and winked at me. "You okay? Thirsty?"

I wasn't anything. Not thirsty. Not hungry. Not... anything. "No, I'm okay."

He walked over. Wade stayed asleep, small sounds releasing from his open mouth. Dane checked the monitor. "That's the meds. When we let them up, you're going to be hungry, thirsty, and in pain. So I'll leave it for just a few more minutes. It's hard to knock you out. I think that's a good sign this worked. Super Soldiers are notoriously hard to keep unconscious."

I lifted my wrist and looked at it. It read zero. I gasped, and Wade opened his eyes. "What's wrong?" He grabbed my free hand. "What can I do?" He shook his head. "Someone tell me what's going on?"

I touched his cheek to make him look at me. "It's zero."

"It better fucking be." He shook his head. "Dane, where is the readout?" He got to his feet. "I don't see it."

"On my tablet where it will remain not your business for the moment. You were out cold. I don't trust you to take care of her right now. When was the last time you slept? Don't tell me. I can imagine. I didn't sleep for a decade, worrying about Melissa. And then there was the time I thought she was dead. That was about eight months. That was a special kind of hell."

Wade's face fell. "I don't ever want to know that pain."

"Nope, you don't." He patted Wade on the arm. "Sit down. And be her guy, or I'm going to let those men in here. I think they're only obeying because it suits them to believe it's a good thing for her. Otherwise, they'd bust down the door. I've seen it with Sterling. I don't know how it is with five of them, but I can imagine. You know what?" He snapped his fingers. "That's a good idea. You need a break.

Go get a shower and some food. Then come back. Let one of them in."

The door flung open, and Corbin strode in fast. How had he beat the others out? I smiled. It didn't matter. I was glad to see whichever one of them wanted to be here.

"Son." Dane stopped him with a word. "She is going to be in a lot of pain any second. If you're not the guy to endure that silently while being supportive, go get another one of her loves. I'm that guy for Melissa. Cooper is not. We all have our strengths. He gives her better advice. So, are you? That guy?"

Corbin visibly swallowed. I'd never seen him thrown like he looked in that second. Dane had thrown him off his game. He stood slightly straighter. "Sir, I can be whoever she needs me to be. You saved her life. I heard it. When things went a little bit sour, you and Wade saved her. Whatever you tell me to do, I'll do it. I'm going to get my ass kicked when I leave her because I just strode in while they started to debate who it should be. So, yes, I'm that guy."

"Good." Dane dragged Wade to the door and pushed him through it. "The painkillers are about to disappear. Then we'll see how it went. We know it cured her, but what were the other consequences? That is about to be judged."

If I'd been capable of feeling anxiety in that moment, I was sure I'd be swimming in it.

"Saved me?" I let Corbin take my hand. "Did you almost lose me?"

"The nanos seem to have objected to you not being an infant. They had to be messed with. There were some problems. The doctors? They were great."

That was good to know. They'd taken great care of me. Of course, when the first round of pain hit me, I couldn't think of that at all. I shut my eyes. It didn't help. "Why does it hurt?"

"We redid your system. Forced it. Made you healthy, but in the process, we may have also changed you all the way down to your cells. We'll see." Dane patted my shoulder. "If you start to notice anything other than the pain, please let me know."

I laughed. It wasn't funny, but sometimes laughter is the only thing I could do. I discovered that fact in that second. "Like what?"

"Like if you can suddenly hear Corbin's heart. I want to know that."

I tried to see if I could. Only, I couldn't do anything but breathe. I'd have to figure out if I could hear his heart later. It was enough that in that moment I could hold his hand. Being there for me was exactly what I needed. In the pain, I wasn't alone. Thank goodness.

BLAZE MASSAGED the muscles in my lower back, and I moaned with relief. I was constantly tense, and it led to a forever feeling of being in pain. That would pass, we hoped. No one really knew what was going to happen with me. I wasn't sick—the zero in my arm held steady, so much so that Wade wanted to take the device out soon—but I wasn't right yet. The question was, would I ever be. My father had just left The Farm to go get my mother and bring her here. I'd almost gotten used to having him around, but I didn't notice his absence either. I'd gone my whole life without him, although I appreciated he was trying now.

"And you can't hear it?" Kellan stood across from where I sat on the couch, mostly braced in Blaze's lap. They'd taken to constantly rubbing my sore spots, and I was forever grateful. "My heartbeat?"

That was another thing that they kept checking. Had I developed any particularly impressive new talents? The answer seemed to be no. Wade was hugely relieved about this because it meant he hadn't messed up when he'd done the procedure, but even though they didn't say it, I was pretty sure it disappointed the Super Soldiers. As for Trenton, he seemed to be mostly concerned with the fact that I was still, a week later, in pain.

I shook my head. "Sorry, no heartbeat. Does it still beat for me, Kellan?"

Okay, that was silly to say, but he liked it when I did that. His cheeks heated up red for brief seconds and that gave me never-ending amounts of joy. Teasing Kellan into happiness seemed to be partially my job. We still didn't know if I could zap people or open up and take emotion yet. No one was asking me to try, but we would before Wade took out the indicator in my arm.

For now, there was just Blaze, his strong hands, and Kellan's questioning stare. Blaze found a particularly sore spot, and I jumped.

"Easy." His voice was barely a whisper in my ear. "It's good for you."

I nodded. Well, we thought it was. The whole no-one-really-knew-what-they-were-doing-with-me problem continued to rage. Amber had come and checked me out a few times, as had all the other doctors regularly. They had a lot of collective confusion. I was trying not to focus on it. No one wanted their doctors to be so unknowing.

Corbin strode into the room, setting down the equipment he carried on the table. He'd been working on Artemis, a lot. Although we had no plans to go anywhere anytime soon, it seemed like my guys had taken the attitude that they'd broken Artemis and it was, therefore, their collective responsibility to fix her.

"How's it going?" I smiled at him, and he grinned back at me.

"Should be done soon. It would be fixed, but Tommy Sandler had thoughts on how to make her stronger, and so we had to undo and redo. He's smart, good at what he does. Kind of a pain in the ass but driven. It's complicated. Should we be upgrading her when she's really probably going to be retired and never put out to space again?"

My heart clenched. Was it really time to put that ship to bed? How did that even work? I was making rapid progress in how much I understood, or at least functioned with, technology, but that didn't mean I understood the ins and outs of everything. How did they judge when her time was up?

"Would they retire her here?" I reached forward and took a sip of the water. That was another thing. I was supposed to hydrate, hydrate, hydrate. I'd drunk so much liquid at this point I was pretty sure I might float away in a river called Sienna.

Corbin shook his head. "There's talk about giving her back to Melissa on Mars Station. She was her ship on the other side of the galaxy. There are legends about it, or so I heard. No one ever told us those kinds of stories."

I had to pee. All the liquid made that happen, a lot. I turned in Blaze's lap. "Give me a second. Bathroom break."

"Yep." He let go of me. "Are you hungry? Kellan could make another grilled cheese."

The red rose in Kellan's cheeks again. "That's not funny. I didn't mean to burn it. I will get better at it."

Blaze shook his head. "I just thought there was nothing you could fail at. Except, apparently, toasting cheese and butter on bread."

I left them to their back and forth. It had become comforting. If they were knocking at each other gently, it meant they were all okay. When one of them went quiet, that was a different deal altogether. Something was wrong.

Using the bathroom fast, I did start to think about that grilled cheese. Maybe I would make it for them. Surely my muscles could handle that much use. I could get back and forth to the shower, back and forth to the bathroom. I could handle standing at the stove. I sighed. Being weak really made me appreciate the things I used to just do without much thought.

Did I need a nap?

I shuffled out of the bathroom and abruptly stopped. Standing in the room was Canyon and Ari. They stared at me. Something about them didn't look right.

Maybe it was the fact that Ari's hair was short and Canyon's longer. I'd just seen both of them in the last week. How was that possible?

Time travel. Yes, they were somehow involved in that. The secret that somehow everyone knew about because you couldn't keep secrets around Super Soldiers.

"What's wrong?"

Canyon held the door handle and turned away from me to hold the door. "I've got it, but they'll be through very fast."

Ari strode toward me. "Sienna, all is not well. We aren't able to keep Evander out of here very long. They figure out that black hole again and again. They have to be stopped. And I'm afraid it has to be you."

"Me?" They had to be kidding. "I'm not capable of stopping anyone from doing anything." I pointed to the door. "Go talk to them."

"Well, obviously I am. They can hear me, and they've all figured out I'm not from this time and that I'm not here to hurt you. Or at least I hope they figured that out. I'd never hurt you. You're Waverly's best friend, and our kids are best friends."

Kids? My mouth fell open.

"Ari," Canyon huffed. "Back on track."

"Millions of people are going to die. Billions. It doesn't stop. But you... you have the ability to stop all of this. Wade knows more than he's telling you at this point. He's known for days that you're stronger and more powerful than you've ever been. And he thinks that Kellan knows it, too."

Canyon snorted. "Well, that got their attention off her."

"You said to tell you that you had this dream. That you know you have to go through the black hole and that you have to do what you set out to do. You have to do it so that no more people get hurt."

That sounded remarkably like me. I stepped toward him, practically creaking when I did. "How am I supposed to do any of that? And why not just tell me in whatever time you're from?"

"By the time we figure it out, it's too late. I'm sorry to do this. I'd never hurt you, but we don't have time for this to happen on its own. The first attack comes tonight. Warn Diana to put up the shields." He pulled a needle out of his pocket, and I winced. Really? More? Needles?

Hadn't I had enough?

Ari jammed it in my arm. "Just a steroid. But it's going to wake everything up. There was a reason Evander never made female Super Soldiers. Turns out estrogen works really well to block all the devices they've made to control your male counterparts." Canyon backed up from the door just as Ari finished speaking. "See you soon."

They popped out of the room, and the door crashed open, coming off its hinges. Anders ran to me. When had he gotten here?

Dizziness passed before my eyes, and I sank to my knees. Funny thing though, my aching muscles didn't hurt so much anymore.

His arms came around me quickly. "Get Wade. And Ari." He spoke to the others. "Fast."

I shook my head. "I doubt the Ari of now knows anything about what happened."

Kellan sighed. "No, he doesn't. He's just going about his day. But... tell me something, Sienna, can you hear my heartbeat?"

Lub-Dub, Lub-Dub.

I stared up at him. "I..."

Lub-Dub, Lub-Dub. Then again. Lub-Dub, Lub-Dub. But that time not from him. No, that time it was from Anders. Then Blaze who stood in the doorway. But they sounded slightly different from one another. And there were more. So many more. Over and over. I covered my ears.

Kellan nodded. "It's a lot when you're not used to it."

How did they ever think, ever function when there was so much noise everywhere? I covered my ears with my hands. What had Ari done to me? How did they expect me to do anything when there were so many heartbeats everywhere? I couldn't help anyone. This was too much.

Anders squeezed me. "The reason you could take the nanos was because you can control your brain functions better than most people can. Remember what your dad told you about how your brain works? You slow down yours regularly. When I don't want to hear heartbeats, I simply choose not to. Takes a little work, but you can do it too. You can filter things out. The nanos are rewriting you to make you more like us. That's all."

That was all? I had to force myself to think, to focus. A headache formed in the middle of my forehead. "How do I filter the sounds?"

Blaze knelt down in front of me. "When we used to

teach the juveniles how to do this, we used to tell them that some of it is visualization until you get used to it, and then your brain will just do it. So let's try that. Picture a filter."

I listened to his words, a pressing thought overriding the advice he was giving. "Blaze, an attack tonight."

"I know. Devil is telling Diana now. Don't worry on that. Listen to me. Just my words."

Kellan pounded his hand on the wall, denting it. "I'm going to kill Ari."

"They must have good reason." Anders shook his head. "I don't believe they'd endanger her for no reason. In fact, we have to leave for the black hole immediately and do some of this on the ship. I don't know if we have time to wait if it were so important they came back in time."

None of that could concern me right now. I had to picture a filter, I had to listen to Blaze because I couldn't continue like this. It had only just started, but *Lub-Dub, Lub-Dub* would make a person crazy.

* * *

Much of the next few hours were a blur. Artemis must have been space-ready, because we were on her before nightfall as The Farm braced for an assault. Mars Station was so confused. They'd had no indication that anyone or anything had gotten through the black hole, but I guessed they believed the time travelers, because they were moving fast despite whatever reservations they had.

None of that was our problem as we loaded up to go.

"I don't know where the time stream device is." A muscle ticked in Rohan's jaw. "And I never lose anything."

Lub-Dub, Lub-Dub

It was getting better, but it wasn't gone. Rohan's

sounded different than Blaze's. That much was clear. I might have even been able to tell them apart if I concentrated on it. Fuck. I didn't want to. I absolutely did not wish to spend enough time on this that I could tell them apart.

"I have it," Devil volunteered.

All eyes turned to him. It was Rohan who spoke again. "What?"

"I grabbed it for you." He neglected to say why or when he'd done it. "So don't worry about it. Anders is hooking it up now."

Rohan clearly wanted to say more, but Jackson put a hand on his shoulder. "I think you're all ready to go now. Good luck. I mean, you have no plan. We have absolutely no idea how you're going to stop Evander's advancement, but apparently Canyon and Ari think you should be doing this, so off you go. See you again."

Blaze tugged on my hand and grinned at Devil. "You're just pissing people off left and right. The Chens. The Time Travelers. It's amazing how everywhere you go, they get mad."

Devil laughed, and then so did Blaze. No one else in the room was laughing. It was finally Rohan who spoke again. "You know once upon a time, you two used to run things. You kept order. You were in charge. I might think that would be enough for you two to understand that things have to run the way they have to run. And not go around stealing..."

Blaze shook his head. "We ran things badly. So poorly in fact that you and others pretended to be dead to get away from us. Guess that means others should be in charge. Devil and I do better existing in chaos. Much preferred, actually."

Devil shrugged. "We're basically weapons. Use us the way you want to. We'll do whatever we have to do to protect her. Otherwise we're just glad to be on this ride with her. So go ahead and moralize if you'd prefer. I taught you to steal. If you're this bad at protecting important things, I guess I didn't do a very good job."

There was so much testosterone in here I might throw up from the abundance of it. "Okay. Thank you. We'll be on our way now. Good luck to all of us since, you know, we're all trying to save the universe."

I let Blaze escort me away from the others. That thought jarred me. I let him. The truth was that I could probably pull away from Blaze if I wanted to. I could yank my arm back and he might not have been able to stop me.

Just to see how that would go, if I had the ability, I yanked. It didn't take much effort and I freed myself. Devil stopped walking ahead, turning to watch us.

Blaze lifted his eyebrows. "Did you want your arm back?"

"Not particularly, but I wanted to see if I could get my arm back. Go again? This time don't let go just because I yank. Let's see if I can do it."

He shook his head. "I could end up bruising you. Won't do that."

I took a long, deep breath. "Blaze."

"No, I can't. I'm sorry. Just can't." He shook his head. "I'll never be the reason you carry a mark."

That was sweet, and I loved him for it, but it didn't solve my problem. Devil put out his hand. "Come on. I'll do it."

"You could hurt her."

He nodded. "She's asked for this. I might hurt her, but it won't be a permanent injury. She wants to know how strong she is, if she could get her own wrist back from my grip. I'd like to know that, too. That's a useful thing for all of us to know. Sienna is allowed to risk bruising her own wrist if she wants to."

Blaze shook his head as though that was a ridiculous idea, but I walked over to Devil and put out my wrist. He took it in his grip. It wasn't overly tight. The kind that would say to me that the person holding my wrist meant business but didn't mean to hurt me. Any tighter and that would change.

"Get your arm back." He spoke in a low voice. There was no visible aggression on him. This was still the Devil who had made me come in the gentlest of ways the last time we'd been alone together. "Or don't. I'm happy to hold it forever."

Blaze groaned. "That's a good line. Why can't I ever think of them? I feel them. I just have no ability to speak things like that."

I smiled at him. "I know how you feel."

"Oh, I doubt that very much, but that doesn't matter right now. Go on. Get your arm back from him with as little damage as possible, please."

The same feeling that I'd had with Blaze struck me now. I wasn't stuck unless I wanted to be. It wasn't something I could explain, even to myself. I simply understood that I could overpower this situation should I choose to.

Maybe it wasn't me that Blaze should be worried about.

I yanked my arm, not even particularly hard, and twisted slightly. Devil squeezed, obviously meaning to hang on, but I was faster. In the time it took him to make the attempt, my arm was back at my side.

His mouth fell open, and I stared at him, a smile forming on my face. "Not bruised."

"You could have hurt me there if you'd known how."

Devil still stared at me like a landed fish. "It was another two moves for you to hurt me. Did you sense that?"

I shook my head. "Slightly, I guess, but not really. It was more like the sense that I wasn't going to be hurt. Not so much that I wanted to cause you pain."

Blaze took a step toward us. "Okay. Give me your arm."

I smiled. This had taken an unusual turn. And if nothing else, I really wasn't thinking about anyone's heartbeat. For the first time in a long time, I felt strong. It was possible I'd never felt this way before. Ever.

* * *

I stood next to Wade, watching the ship pull away from orbit. The Farm was behind us, at least for now. Artemis was familiar, and the terror of space travel wasn't striking me this time. He hadn't said very much since we'd boarded.

"You okay?" I bumped into him gently.

"Yep." He responded, not looking in my direction.

I sighed. "How about the truth? I could try to decide if you're lying by paying attention to things you're doing inside like the others do, but I've just managed to start tuning out heartbeats, so if it's all the same to you, I'd rather not."

He looked at me with tired eyes. "I fucked up, or this wouldn't have happened to you."

"I don't think so. What more could you have done to prevent it? Maybe it was inevitable."

Wade rubbed his eyes. "I don't accept that. I'm not fatalistic, time travel aside. I could have done something else."

He was beating himself up pretty heavily. "Is that why

you didn't mention anything? Because you thought it was your fault? Or you were trying to fix it?"

Wade dropped his hand and linked our fingers. "Maybe I didn't want to see the hate in your eyes."

"Take a deeper look, Wade. That's not how I feel about you. Not even a little bit."

He cupped the side of my cheek. "How do you feel about me?"

I kissed him. It was hard for me to initiate affection. Maybe it was all of my years going without. But Wade didn't seem to want to start it up either. Perhaps we were more alike than we weren't. His lips were warm, and the scruff on his cheeks cut at me. I actually liked the pinch of pain.

"I'm in love with you." I swallowed. "Are you in love with me? You saved my life. Whatever else happened, it's not on you."

Breathing hard, he pressed his forehead against mine. "I'm not worthy of you like these men are. I got kidnapped. Taken from my family. They were tormented because of me. I can't even look at them. And you are now going to have to live this existence you never should have had to have because of my incompetence, and what's more, I could have let any of the others do it. I insisted it had to be me because—"

I interrupted him. "Because I'm yours. I am yours. And thank goodness it was you. I almost died, right? Dane said you saved my life. I am grateful for everything about you. We've all made mistakes. Big ones. You being taken and abused by Evander is not one of them."

I almost asked Wade to make love to me right there. But I didn't think he was the public, up-against-the-window type.

"Can you come to my room tonight? Just you and me? And maybe we could show each other how much we love each other. What do you think?"

His pulse jumped. I actually heard it. Yes, I was pretty sure he liked the idea very much. I breathed out. I needed to stay present and not in my head, thinking about the sounds other people made. I wanted to be here with Wade. That was the most important thing I could do right now.

I kissed his chin. "You like that idea."

"I do. Yes, I'd like to come tonight. You and me. I'm thinking about all the ways I can show you that I love you."

I lifted an eyebrow. "Naked."

He visibly gulped. I didn't even have to hear it. "Naked."

"How about if we pretend it's night right now?"

My love nodded. He certainly seemed to have lost the use of words. I took his hand and drew him with me to my room. I hadn't unpacked, but at least I had a few things to put around this time. A toothbrush and some changes of clothes. Actually, there were more things than I'd had in here. A very nice lamp and some pretty pictures of sunny days on the wall.

It took me a second to realize what had happened. "Diana and Waverly."

"They both lived on this ship." Wade kissed the side of my neck. I shivered. Yes, I liked his lips there very much. "Maybe they wanted to make it seem more like home since we're going to be in the black hole for a really long time."

I wrapped my arms around his neck. "Well, then we'll have lots of time for this kind of a thing."

His heart beat faster, and I smiled. Maybe there were some benefits to being able to hear it. I kissed him lightly on the chin, the side of his face. "You didn't break me, Wade.

I'm right here. Strong. I don't feel wrong. So how about you forgive yourself and not hold on to this pain? I could try to take the pain from you if you want."

He widened his eyes. "No, don't do that. Don't ever do that. I felt that once. And Super Soldier powers or no Super Soldier powers, I'd prefer you never do that again."

We both knew that wasn't going to happen. I'd have to do it sooner than later to make sure I still could and that it didn't affect the virus level. But not now. For just these moments, I wanted to be alone with Wade, both of us alive and healthy.

That was a gift he'd given me. One of many. This man kept saving my life.

"I know you said no fatalism." He kissed the end of my nose as I spoke. "But it seems like a lot of things happened to bring us together, Wade. Maybe all of it had to happen to be here in this moment. Maybe it was all meant to be."

He drew me even closer. I could have heard his heart beat even if I didn't have these newly acquired abilities. "Sweet words, Sienna. I'm going to hold on to them. If anyone could make me a glass-half-full guy, it would be you."

WADE'S LIPS WERE WARM, his breath sweet and clean, and I fit against him like I'd been made to do so every day of my life. How could he doubt that there was some sort of meaning behind all of us, some sort of meant to be? Or maybe I'd just spent too long living in a temple. The good news about my sudden procedure and subsequent recovery was that I'd not had to deal with seeing the people who thought I was a religious figure in the Dark Planets. I didn't want to be that woman. No, I simply wanted to be the kind that got to be naked with Wade as much as I wanted. I thought that seemed like a pretty good way to live.

He took control of the kiss. It was gentle but quickly changed. Wade pressed my back into the wall, his caress becoming frantic. He so rarely lost control, but my guess was that was about to change. He roamed his hands over the top of my clothes, squeezing my nipples, pinching them through the fabric. I gasped in his mouth, and he drank down the sound.

"You like that?" He pinched harder. "Tell me when it's too much."

I didn't know if there would be such a thing with him. Too much? What was that? There could never be enough. I'd been frozen, literally in some ways, and this man had thawed me out.

Wade. I spoke in his head because I knew how much he liked that

His body shuddered against mine. "You make me shaky when you do that. Like I could melt into a puddle of heat and be glad for having done so."

"I reached for you in my sleep before I ever knew you. You were already there, already in my heart. Already mine."

He spun me around, laying me down on the bed. Both of us were already breathing hard. Staring down at me, he seemed to be searching my face for something. "You want this."

It wasn't a question, but it was a chance for me to change my mind. This man would always put others' needs above his own. He would always seek the right thing to do. It was just how he was made, and it killed me a little inside that he didn't see himself that way.

I kissed him hard, and he smiled in return. Wade sat up a little and threw his shirt over the side of the bed. "I'm dying to feel you skin-to-skin."

I wanted the same, so I followed suit and disrobed so that he could see me beneath my shirt. I was actually wearing a bra, a feat that hadn't been going on for so long because of how constantly I went without the right clothing. But I had what I needed, for now. The undergarment was pink and lacy, not the most comfortable one I owned. Still, the way he stared at the lingerie made me glad I'd put it on.

He ran his hand over my stomach once then twice. "So beautiful." He bent down and kissed the area of skin between my breasts and my abdomen. "So soft."

I ran my hands through his hair. He was always so well put together, but right now, for Wade, he looked downright scruffy. "I don't think of myself as soft."

"Well, you are." He kissed me again before he unhooked my bra in the front. "If I had known you were wearing that bra—that pink lace—I would have been hard all day thinking about it. It's like an innocent device that is covering up your sexy heat beneath."

He took my nipple in his mouth and sucked on it. A moan left his mouth—deep, scorching. To know he wanted me this much was powerful, beautiful. Humbling. I craved him too, but I was comfortable with the idea. Wade had told me he didn't deserve me. To even be here with me, he was overcoming something deep and profound.

I was grateful he'd taken the leap.

I ran my hands through his hair, watching him love on my breast. There was something so erotic about that, and I was sure I'd take this image with me to my dying breath. Wade lost, giving me pleasure. Little jolts of it rolled through in me waves. It would build and waver. I squirmed as it increased, wanting more than what he was giving me but not wanting to lose the moment. Was it possible to grasp a memory and insist it stay fresh forever?

"Wade. Let me kiss you." He lifted his head, and I lost myself when his mouth met my own. There was nothing better than this. The moment. The sharing of breath. We would be closer when our bodies were joined, but there was an intimacy to this that wouldn't be shared in that. A kiss, especially with Wade, was a promise of forever. A loving. It was the first step in how we would give ourselves to each other.

I cupped him on the outside of his pants and felt how he grew beneath the fabric. It had to be hurting, but he didn't seem to mind. He ground into my hand, and then sighed against my lips. When he lifted his head, he was grinning at me.

"I half-expect to wake up and find this is just another dream I'm having about you."

I grinned. "This is very real, my love."

We stripped each other the rest of the way. It was slow, unhurried. I didn't feel like the world was about to explode. It might do that, but I wouldn't live that way, not when I had times like this to be with this man. I wanted to own his seconds, live his years. He'd given me this opportunity, and I intended to treasure the moments.

When we were finally bare, I couldn't stop staring at him. Wade was lean and muscular. I traced my fingers over the lines on his chest. He let me for a bit before he pulled me onto his lap. I straddled him. This was different for me. I'd not made love quite like this before. He was on his knees, and when he was inside of me, I imagined he would be as close to me as was humanly possible.

I lifted myself up and with his help, came down on him, letting him inside of me when I did. We both gasped, and he closed his eyes. "Like a glove."

If he wasn't making one hundred percent sense, that was fine. I couldn't imagine I was either. It was hard to figure out the movements. I didn't want to entirely pull out of him, but this wasn't the easiest thing to do. Until I learned how this should go. Arching my back, I pulled down and pressed out until every movement took me over my clit.

We would both cry out when I did that. I bit down on my lip. They'd hear us all the way back on the planet we'd left, we were being so loud. Then I gave up doing that. What did I care? Let everyone in the universe know how much I loved Wade, how glad I was to have his heart. To share his body in this time that was ours.

He lifted his hips, and I rode him harder. This was messy, wet, and so fucking glorious. On and on we moved; I almost fell over, but he grabbed me. No one would call this graceful, but I didn't care. I loved every second of it. And the new angle really worked for me. I let go of where I held on to his shoulders and leaned all the way back, letting him support me. And then I was done.

I came. Hard. My body convulsed, and then so did my mind. There was only Wade, his beautiful soul, and the way that we made each other feel.

He kissed me all over my face, murmuring things, but I could hardly hear him over the fog that descended on me. Pleasure fled gradually, and in its place, a slowness that made everything seem hazy.

We lay down together, separating for the first time. I was going to need a shower. A big one. But not now. I wanted to roll around feeling like this for a while.

If I could move at all.

"Yours. Always." He rolled me against his chest. I could hear his heartbeat without even having to think about it. But it was the sound of his eyelids closing that caught my attention. Just a flutter of a sound, but there it was.

Wade was asleep, fast. I didn't even have to look at him to know. The thought woke me up, jarring away some of that haze. I was sure that someday that would be an old hat thing to notice, but for right now, it was very new. Too singular to ignore by going to bed.

I snuggled closer. He smelled really good. His natural clean scent was altered with a spicy newness that I was pretty sure was me. I kissed his skin, and he shifted slightly but didn't stir.

How far could I hear? I closed my eyes and tried to see what I could notice. It didn't take long before a whoosh told me I'd extended my abilities. The others were in the engine room. Even Trenton, who touched his tablet with a tap-tap-tap. I could actually make out those sounds. I didn't have to see it to know what he was doing.

"Can you make that go faster?" Blaze spoke to someone. "We're going to be in that hole a year. You know how I feel about the hole. It's like hell. Might even make me wish for cryo."

A laugh. Anders. "I'm working on it. I will shave off time. A lot of it. Trust me."

"I always do." Blaze again. "Think Wade will mind if I snuck in and slept with them?"

"I think Wade is out cold," Devil responded. "And that our Sienna is listening. I can hear the change in her brain-waves. Can't you? Hello, Sienna, love."

I gasped. Not only could I hear them, but they could hear me hearing them? All of them laughed except Trenton who groaned and muttered about privacy.

Pulling back my attention from them, I forced myself to stay in the here and now. How did any of them do this?

Wade murmured in his sleep, and it caught my attention. I could obsess, or I could try to be present. There was this beautiful man who had just given me so much pleasure. He was asleep and warm. I cuddled against him, and he drew me closer, sighing. Wade was incredibly beautiful.

I closed my eyes. His heart thumped, and I decided to be grateful for the sound. That meant he was breathing, that meant he was here. The guys said they listened to my heart beat itself to sleep, and I could see why. It was incredibly soothing.

Sometime later, maybe it was nighttime by then, the

door opened and quiet feet entered the room. Both Wade and I stirred, but as I let my lids flutter open to see who it was, I quickly knew the heartbeat. I'd started to be able to tell whose was whose.

Anders kicked off his shoes and crawled in next to me. Wade scooted to make room for him, and soon I was sandwiched between them. A warm beacon of safety and happiness. Artemis shook, and I came fully awake, but Anders kissed my neck.

"It's just the black hole. Wes opened it. They have ships lined up to stop anyone from coming through while we go out. All okay. You'll get used to the flutter. It'll be with us until we get through. Which I may have greatly shortened the time of."

Wade rolled over. "That's nice. Now shut the fuck up. We can all be impressed tomorrow."

I could feel Anders smile against my neck. "He's so grumpy, but to be fair, he hasn't slept in years. Or ever."

That was fair. I closed my eyes.

* * *

Wade's snores woke me in the morning. I squeezed him gently, and he stopped, moving his head into a better position. Anders was still out cold, but now I was fully awake. I pulled my knees up to my chest and placed my head down on them as I yawned myself awake. My strong body wanted to move, almost like it was driving me to get up. Of course, there wasn't much to do, not for me, on this ship.

Anders was silently asleep in the way that the Super Soldiers seemed to be, as though he was afraid to even make noise breathing.

My stomach grumbled, and I needed a shower. The

noise roused Anders who sat back on his elbows, awake and staring at me. "I could try to cook."

I shook my head. "I'll do it. Go back to bed."

"I'm up now."

Wade groaned. "So am I. How long did we sleep?

Anders threw his feet over the side of the bed. "You slept for almost twelve hours. I think I was more like five, but that is a lot for me, and she has to be rip-roaring ready to go because twelve is practically a week for us."

That was true. Was I really not going to be sleeping?

Wade stretched, getting out of the bed and grabbing his underwear on the way. I was fully naked, and the truth of that hit me all at once. I was totally bare, and they were both in here. I grabbed the sheet and pulled it over myself. Maybe I shouldn't have been embarrassed. I'd been naked with both of them at this point. They'd seen what was under the sheet, but it was a little bit weird.

Anders lifted his eyebrows slowly. "Go get your shower, gorgeous."

"I'm going to have to drug all of you if we're in here a year. You're all going to go crazy." Wade pulled on his shirt. "I'm sort of serious. I didn't consider how long this trip was going to be for everyone but Trenton and me."

Anders walked over to the window. "Yep, it's the vast nothingness I remember. Not that I was awake very much in the Hole. They put us in cryo for just the reason that Wade is discussing. Can't have a bunch of Super Soldiers with nothing to do. However, I've shortened the trip so it should be significantly less time, and we have to train our girl so that she can kill the Evander CEO."

I hadn't thought about that element to this. Stop them, yes. Of course that meant I was going to kill him. Or them. Wasn't there a whole board of directors that was a problem? I'd never killed anyone. Sure, I probably physically could now, but was I going to be able to do this?

Both of the guys stared at me. Had I made a sound, or did I just look as sick as I suddenly felt?

Anders put his arms around me, and I squeezed him back. I was officially a hugger. I'd never wanted to be. It had too much to do with me taking people's pain, but when the guys did it, they seemed to want to comfort as much as they wanted to receive that from me. Right now, Anders rocked me gently.

"I shouldn't have said that. You're not going to kill anyone. It was a stupid thing to say. We're going to train you so you know how to be you now. But we'll take care of Evander. That was always on us."

I pressed my forehead into his shoulder. "Ari said I had to do it. Or maybe it was Canyon. The whole time before they injected me is sort of a blur. Like it was out of time, which I guess it was. It has to be me."

"They don't know everything." Anders shook his head. "Trust me. I grew up with Canyon. Literally in the same juvenile hall. I'm smarter than him."

I snorted. These guys and the constant game of testosterone. How did they not drown in it? "I thought it was Kellan who was always bragging about his big IQ."

"Well, from what I hear, the need to brag means you're overcompensating for something." He waggled his eyebrows just as somewhere in the ship, Kellan yelled out hey in response.

I smiled. It was sort of fun to hear the things I used to miss. Even if it came with all the other strange noises. Like being able to constantly hear the engine if I thought about it.

"I'm going to go make some food." Wade touched my arm. "And he's right. I'll kill them before you will."

I left them to go shower and was glad when no one made any moves to get in with me. It wasn't that I didn't love the attention. In fact, I was becoming addicted to it. The more they gave me, the more I wanted it. As though they could help me fill up the hole from my years of giving and never getting back by just the way they loved me. The more they touched, the more I wanted them to do that.

But for now, I needed to feel the water run down my back and just think.

We were headed across the galaxy because two people I barely knew—even though one of them had helped save my life—told me to do so. I had no idea how I was going to stop Evander. None. But it was obviously going to be violent, and all my guys' assurances aside, I couldn't shake the feeling that they were feeding me a line of bullshit.

Yes, I was cursing in my own head. A lot. And I was pretty sure I couldn't blame the nanos.

It was just me.

What was worse was that I was one hundred percent certain that the guys believed what they were saying to me. They thought I wouldn't have to kill anyone. I was a girl from a temple in a place so remote it was sometimes not on star charts. I'd lived in a temple, even more sheltered than the rest of my planet. And even I knew that when this was over, I would be covered in blood.

The water splashed down on me. Was it possible to pre-wash the sin away? Could I stand here in the shower for however long it took me to get across the galaxy and just flush the whole thing off me now? Build up a resistance?

I sunk to the floor.

The sound of footsteps approaching gave me plenty of

warning that someone else was coming if I wanted to keep them away. But I didn't want to anymore. Being alone meant I had to deal with these plaguing thoughts, and I wasn't going to have answers to them anytime soon.

Anders' heartbeat told me it was him seconds before he drew back the curtain. "I'll never be able to say I'm sorry enough for that stupid thing I said."

I looked up at him, not even caring that the water got into my eyes. "It wasn't stupid. It was honest. Don't take it back and don't apologize. I think you did me a favor. Much better to deal with this now and get the horror over with before I have to do it."

"Do you think I'm going to let you kill people?" He stepped into the spray, fully dressed. "I'd die for you first."

I stood, gripping his rapidly soaking shirt. "Don't say things like that."

"I would. I'd die for you right this second and consider myself a lucky man for having done it. I got to love you, I got to be with you. Those aren't things I should ever have had. I got to make love to you. Gifts that a person like me doesn't get to experience. I don't deserve it. Not one of us on this ship does. And yet you chose us and continue to do so."

I opened my mouth, but he wasn't done yet.

"When we were on The Farm, it occurred to me that you could meet others. I guessed that could happen at any time, but when we were alone on the ships, you were ours, almost by default, but there were a ton of men in those places you might have liked better."

I shoved his shoulder. "Anders."

"Almost done. It then occurred to me that you wouldn't do that. Because you really are like us, heart and soul. When you decide on something, you walk that line. You picked us the same time we picked you. You'd never look to someone else. Yet, I can't help but feel gratitude that you decided on me. I'll always feel that way, and if I die today making sure that you go on to have a beautiful life, I'll end this life knowing that it was the greatest gift that I got any time with you at all."

I was on him fast. I had to have Anders right there in the shower, and since his strength would match my own, I didn't give a thought to overdoing anything. I ripped his clothes from his body. It wasn't even hard. That should have amused me if I wasn't too focused on needing him inside of me right then and there.

"Hard," I told him and meant it. He spread my legs and pushed his finger against my clit. I rubbed myself on his finger. That was great but not what I wanted. "Anders." I was sure he understood.

He smiled before he bit down on my shoulder. "Breathe. I want it, too. I promise you that. Touching you is a rare pleasure. I need it. For just a second."

Anders needed me? I caught my breath. Yes, he could have whatever he wanted. It was just a few more moments that he stroked my clit. I was panting for it by the time he pushed himself inside of me. I threw my head back. That's what I'd wanted. Hard. Just him. Deep inside. Yes, more.

We rode each other in the shower. "Harder." There was no way he could hurt me. I could take whatever it was that he had inside of him. Wanted it. Craved the need. Over and over. The curtain to the shower was gone, the water everywhere. I wasn't even sure how we'd done that except that we were throwing everything into this moment.

Driving it until we might actually explode the bathroom itself by the time we were done.

And then it was over in a long sigh that was so beautiful it brought tears to my eyes. Anders came at exactly the same time I did. His arms were around me. This man with his beautiful words, who could destroy the world, brought peace to my soul.

Yes, he could kill anyone for me. That didn't mean I would let him. He was mine as much as I was his.

THE DAYS PASSED QUICKLY, considering how little there really was for us to do. Anders hadn't been kidding when he said they were going to train me. I got about half a day of that every day before their minds would turn to more amorous thoughts altogether. Well, almost all of them. It was sort of like Kellan and Corbin were avoiding that.

They hadn't even taken to whatever the sleep rotation was proving to be. I didn't know whose turn anything was and hadn't asked, but it seemed like I started most nights with one of them in my bed and ended it with two, sleeping. I didn't need the rest, but it was becoming my favorite part of any day. I forced myself into the dream world because waking up from it with two of them cuddling me was such a treat.

Blaze, Devil, and Anders had to be doing the same thing since they couldn't need any more sleep than I did. Still, I heard no complaints.

"Higher." Kellan ordered me. We'd turned one of the ship bays into a training room, and today Kellan was working on getting me to jump. All strength aside, they were all bigger than I was. The nanos hadn't made me taller or broader. In this particular case, his insistence that I should be able to jump as high as he did was ridiculous and rapidly pissing me off.

"That's as high as I'm going to be able to jump." Not to mention I'd jammed my hip into the side of the wall because the nanos hadn't made me any less clumsy. I could go up just fine, but coming down, I really wasn't graceful.

Kellan walked to the window, staring at the true nothing out there. "Yes, you can. Jump higher, or I'm going to think you need more push-ups to work on your core strength."

I almost told him to go fuck himself. But this was Kellan, and he would probably like that. He'd always marched to the beat of his own drum. From moment one of meeting him when he'd made me so mad I'd zapped him, I hadn't one hundred percent understood him.

I wasn't sure he really understood himself.

Instead, I did something I'd not done in a long time. I opened up my mind, and I sent him a jolt. He yelped before he turned around. A smile crossed his face. Yep, there was Kellan. Always a little off. In the best possible way.

"You did it."

Yes, it seemed I was still capable of it. In fact, the act had felt entirely the same. The only difference being I didn't feel like I had to sit down and rest now. I stepped toward him, and he rushed over to me, grabbing my wrist. I'd not even thought about it, but he was right. We should check the number. I'd been staying at zero, but I hadn't taxed my mind using my abilities in the weeks since we'd changed me.

It still read zero. Kellan nodded like it said something to him. "Can you do it harder?"

I blinked. "You want a stronger zap? I was just poking at you because I knew you liked it."

"I want to see what you can do, and I want you to do it to me."

I shook my head. "That's something I do to hurt people. It's defensive. I'm not going to zap you until I do some kind of permanent brain damage just to see if I can. We'll have to save that and hope for the best if I ever have to do it on an enemy."

"I could survive whatever you dished out."

That deserved an eye roll, so that was what he got. "Do you not want to have sex with me? I mean... if you don't want to, that is fine. I just want to understand what we are. You made a lot of declarations, but maybe you've changed your mind."

He strode so close to me I could feel his breath on my face. "You haven't asked me to sleep with you. Corbin either. It's polite to wait until the lady asks."

I put my hands on my hips. "Ask? I haven't gone around asking. That's not how this has worked. And what's more, you know that because you listen to everything." In other circumstances, that would be weird, even creepy, but not with all of us. It was just understood someone always had an ear listening. I'd found myself doing it a lot. When I washed dishes, I tuned into whoever piloted the ship. It was almost impossible not to.

"Just because they're not obeying general laws of courtesy doesn't mean I won't. Corbin agrees."

I took a long breath. "Kellan, if you want to get your head out of your ass at any time and let us get to know each other in the primal sense of the word, come find me. Otherwise it will be a cold day in hell before I ask for it."

I stormed out of the room, not sure I could have

explained why that pissed me off as much as it did. Maybe it was because it was Kellan. I might not have gotten so angry at Corbin. But Kellan liked to push my buttons. That was how we related. It had almost seemed normal to just press back at him rather than soothe.

My telling him that it was all fine would not have gotten what I wanted from this. Corbin, I could believe he thought he was following some kind of rule where I had to ask for it, but Kellan just wanted to make me squirm. And I wasn't in the mood. I'd jumped as high as I was going to for the time being.

* * *

Being of superior strength and immunity plus all the other amazing things I could now do was great. That didn't, however, mean that I didn't sometimes hurt. At the end of each day, I was sore. Today, brutally so.

After my encounter with Kellan, I'd worked out some more but mostly managed to avoid the others. My guess was they were giving me a wide berth. Why should they want to get their heads snapped off the way Kellan had?

Hours later, my temper had cooled replaced by embarrassment. I was going to have to apologize. Why had I done that? It was like I couldn't be my best self around him, and most of the time I preferred that. With Kellan, it was nice to have someone love me despite the fact that I showed him so consistently just how wicked I could be.

Mean. Petty. Rude. And...

The door swung open. He stood there staring at me. I was in a white bathrobe. We'd brought about a dozen of them with us on the ship, and I wore this one almost every night after I showered when I had to make the pain in my muscles go away.

"I'm sorry." I said the words. "You didn't deserve that."

"Which part?" He threw his shirt against the wall, walking toward me in all his untoward gloriousness.

I rose. "All of it."

"You like to yell at me, and I like that you do. I don't want you to be polite. I just wanted you to ask me to fuck you. I wanted you to want it that much. Yes, that's a selfish, dickish move, but that is what we do for each other. We give each other the space to be base and screwed up. I spend too much time during the day pretending to be normal. I like that I don't have to be with you." He stood close again. Like earlier, I could feel him breathe.

For the fun of it, I zapped him, lightly, again. He widened his eyes before he kissed me hard, biting on my lower lip until he drew blood. I backed up, wide-eyed. Damn. I loved that.

I bounced on my feet, not sure why, but there was a definite adrenaline boost to my system.

"Like that?"

"You know what, Kellan?" Was I really going to do this? Yes, I was. I sure was.

He lifted an eyebrow. "What?"

I shoved him backward with a hard zap. "Catch me. If you think you can."

And then I was off. I couldn't say where the need came from. I'd never had it before, but I wanted to run, and more than that, I needed to see if Kellan could catch me. Had I possessed this desire before? I had no idea. I'd spent my life locked up in a temple. Maybe I had, maybe I hadn't. I'd blame the nanos if I had to, but I didn't really care.

I was in a bathrobe, wearing no shoes, and rushing

through Artemis like I was in some childhood game that hopefully would end with both of us naked.

If he was strong enough to catch me.

I rushed through the ship, nearly colliding with Devil, who had the good sense to hit the wall. I opened up my senses just as Dev grabbed my arm. "Don't make it so easy on him."

What did he mean? He passed me the device that he used to hide me from the guys when he'd abducted me from Mars Station. We'd used it on Trenton to hide him from the Evander soldiers, too. I grinned at him, putting it on my wrist.

With a nod, I took off even though, from behind me, I heard Kellan curse. Yep, we'd just made this much more of a chase. I ran as hard and as fast as I could, trying to keep silent as I did. Eventually, I made my way to a bay that I was told had once grown fruits and vegetables. I couldn't remember who had used it that way. This ship had so many people who had run it, I couldn't keep track from one story to another of who did what.

I didn't really care. Right now, the bay was filled with cartons that were filled with things to fix the engines and repair parts of Artemis should we need it. More like a storage warehouse. I grabbed a wrench from a box and waited. Eventually, he would find me, and then he was going to have to disarm me, too.

Why I got wet thinking about that was beyond me. It wasn't as though I wanted others to do this. I absolutely did not. In fact, if Anders tried this, it would be strange. But Kellan? Yes, this is what I craved. Find me, Kellan, catch me, and take away my weapon.

I vibrated from wanting it, and staying silent was hard. But it added to the anticipation. I listened for him. He was close. In the right hallway. He took deep breaths. It was like he was searching for me with smell. Why find me by sound if he could follow his nose?

Grinning, I continued to listen. It wouldn't have occurred to me to do that. But then I'd never had to use these newfound abilities in battle, never had to try them. Maybe Kellan had to use his nose before.

I could run again, but now I wanted to fight. So I stood there. And I waited for him.

He didn't let me down.

The door flung open, and he stood in the precipice, waiting for a second. Framed by the light, he looked huge and strong. My mouth watered.

He scanned the room for me, but I wasn't hidden, just waiting in the corner.

"Take the device off. I need to hear you."

It was the need that got me. I took it off and set it aside. Kellan nodded a second later and for one brief moment closed his eyes. "Not hearing you is painful." A muscle pulsed in his jaw. "But now that we've taken care of that." He strode toward me. "Oh, she holds a wrench. How quaint."

I loved his tone like this. Cold and yet filled with heat. Kellan was a predator. I wanted to be his prey. But he had to earn it.

"Think you can take it from me?"

He smirked. "Blaze hasn't taught you weaponry yet. You're holding that like you want to stir soup with it."

Was I? I looked down at the wrench, and he was on me, throwing the wrench over his head to the side. It hit the wall with a clank, and we were both on the ground, him on top of me. "You'll learn soon enough, if we hit that level of train-ing, that distraction works as well as anything else. It's basic but effective. When was the last time you stirred soup? Ever? Why would you know how to do that?"

So he'd tricked me. It was sort of sexy. Or nothing sort of about it. "You caught me."

"I'll always catch you. I'll always find you. That is what I do. And thank you for this. Sometimes I get so tired of having to try to be human. I'm not ever going to be just like them. It's exhausting spending all that time trying to be."

I tilted my head. "Who said you have to be exactly like everyone else?"

"Not you." He kissed me gently. The hard press of the lips didn't come. Instead, he planted kisses all over my face. Caresses like he was afraid he might hurt me with his mouth. "I caught you. I get to keep you now. I get to worship your body, because you are going to let me. Do you understand?"

I nodded. Yes, I did. And it was exactly what I wanted. "Yes."

"Good. You're such a beautiful doll right now. Mine to play with."

The rougher and more demanding his words became, the more opposite his movements were. I'd never felt more treasured or taken care of. He kissed down my body, removing my robe as he did. We were on the floor, but it felt soft, like I was on a bed.

"You need me to take care of you right now."

I nodded. I absolutely did. "Yes."

I was fully naked, and he was still totally dressed. But he'd handle that. I knew he would. If he wanted me to touch him, he'd have to take off his clothes.

"Put your hands over your head and keep them there. For now."

I nodded. We'd never done this together before, but it

felt like we had, there was that level of comfort with him. The newness was there, sure, but also this inherent trust in him. He'd caught me. Oh, how it turned out I'd needed that. I put my hands over my head. Somehow, he'd earned the right to tell me to do that.

And I loved it.

He dropped his head at about the same second that he pushed my knees apart. I didn't have time to clench or think about it before his mouth was on my pussy. I shuddered. Kellan licked and sucked in just the right places. What was more, he really seemed to relish the sensation. He moaned and sighed, breathing me in while he did it.

I arched beneath him, unable to stop the movement of my body. He put his hand higher on my knee but otherwise didn't stop me. I would stop if Kellan told me to. I'd find a way, but he didn't, and so I could move as I wanted.

In no time at all, I writhed against him. It was close. So close. But not enough. I couldn't quite get what I needed. I didn't know why. My clit throbbed. My body begged for relief. It was just not happening.

"I want you to come."

With an unexpected ease, I did. Sometimes it was so nice to be told what to do. Now was one of those moments. He held my legs while I let go, feeling the wave of the orgasm he'd brought me. My breasts ached and my insides begged for more.

He pulled his shirt off, followed by his pants. Kellan had scared me the first time I saw him. Not anymore. Sure, he was lethal, but he was my lethal man.

Kellan took my hand and placed it on his cock. He was long, hard, thick, and heavily veined. My mouth watered. But he hadn't put my mouth on him, he'd put my hand. I stroked him once, then twice.

"More." He closed his eyes.

I did just as he said, loving every second of this and practically squirming from anticipation. I cupped him on his head and then stroked down all the way to his balls. He let out a long hiss. "That's enough. I just had to feel your hands, so the next time I'm jerking myself off, I can picture yours better. I want you all the time. It's a constant battle to restrain myself."

I lifted an eyebrow. "You waited a long time."

"I'm a jackass, but I love you."

That was quite a confession from him. It was hard for him to say things like that. I bit his chin, and he grinned. He took my hand off him and pushed inside of me. With one hard jerk of his cock, he was balls deep. I gasped and then sighed. Yes, I'd needed this connection. What's more, I was certain he did, too.

We ground at each other, every move a dance of possession. I let him set the rhythm, let him determine the pace. I was happy to follow his lead. This was Kellan. He was mine, and I was his. This was how things should be between us.

Minutes went on until I could hardly breathe from the pressure building inside of me. With a final jerk against my clit, I came. It was blissful. It was perfect. It was everything I could have hoped it would be.

We breathed against each other, gasping for air. Finally, Kellan picked up his head. "You're going to have a burn on your back from the floor. I'm sorry. We could have found a softer place."

I shook my head. "Whatever. It'll heal, and I've never wanted anything as much as what just happened between us right here. This was how it was supposed to be between us."

He kissed me gently. "Wasn't too much?"

"No such thing." I sat up, achy. Yes, it was going to be a night where I hurt. "Thanks for this."

Snorting, he kissed all over my face. "Don't thank me. And I'll be in your bed tonight. There's a rotation. I'm on it now."

I smiled. That sounded perfect.

* * *

My body hurt. It was hard to sleep. Next to me, Kellan dozed easily, but every time I tried to move, my muscles reminded me that despite their newfound power, they weren't used to the kind of straining of them that I'd been doing lately. The door opened and closed. This was routine. The person joining the bed would wait until the other one was out cold to come in. I wasn't sure how Wade and Trenton exactly knew, but they seemed to manage it, too. Tonight, it was Anders.

I could see better in the dark these days, and it was clear to me Anders wasn't moving well. I sat up, ignoring the pain. "You okay?"

He pointed to his head, climbing in next to me. "Headache."

Anders confessed to me a while back that he got headaches, and it was his deepest shame. Super Soldiers didn't get headaches, or Evander put them down. My guess now that I had some of their traits was that more of them than not were hiding ailments. They'd simply learned how to silently handle horrible things.

I wrapped my arms around him. "I'm sorry."

"Hmm." He closed his eyes. "I can leave if this bothers you."

That made little sense. "Why would your headache bother me?"

Kellan rolled over, reaching across me to squeeze Anders' arm. "You're not alone. And you don't have to be that way when you hurt. It doesn't make you weak."

Anders rolled to face us, lying on his side to face both of us. My aching muscles didn't hurt so badly now. I closed my eyes and, with Kellan, held Anders the rest of the night.

I didn't need to sleep, so this time I didn't force myself to do so. Anders slept hard, and I hoped it meant that his headache would pass by morning. Kellan's eyes were closed. He breathed evenly, barely audibly. I didn't want to wake Anders, but the way his face scrunched up in pain made tears come to my eyes.

The poor man. I reached out and stroked my finger over his forehead. He sighed and pressed his head more thoroughly into my hand.

I held him like that, not moving, glad I could offer what little comfort I could to such a strong man.

* * *

Morning came slowly. I didn't feel tired from staying up all night. In fact, I felt better for not forcing it. My muscles were looser, and I could breathe easier.

"You guys better get in here." Blaze's voice sounded in the room although he was across the ship. Kellan's and Anders's eyes flew open at the same time. Anders blinked rapidly but got up, throwing his legs over the bed fast. Kellan had his clothes on by the time I realized what was happening.

Blaze needed our attention. I jumped off the bed and ran toward my dresser. As fast as I could, I threw on my own clothing, stopping only to regard Anders. "You okay?"

"Better than last night."

That didn't mean he was fixed. But I wasn't going to point that out when there wasn't a thing to do about it right now. Fully dressed, we ran down the hall. I needed a shower and food, but comfort could wait if Blaze needed us. Funny, how we'd become an us. I could participate in this.

In the comm room, everyone waited for us. With the exception of Blaze, everyone was half put together. I looked at the clock on the side of Dev's tablet that he held. It was early morning. If they hadn't been sleeping, they hadn't been ready for action either. There were no alarms going off. We were in the Hole. What could be going wrong here?

Blaze spun around in his chair. "I found something."

Trenton scratched his head. "Really? Out here?"

"Yep," he nodded. "The last thing I did before they put us in cryo to carry us across the galaxy was participate in a training exercise on a new ship they were designing." He sighed. "It didn't work. Almost blew us up. But that was a long time ago. Thanks to cryo, the truth is that I have no idea how much time that was. We don't really know how long we were under and waiting to be activated before Waverly woke us up and changed things." He sighed again. "Enough time to develop the ship."

My body went cold. He was really worried about that ship. "Is it out there?"

"Not the exact ship. But clearly a new version."

Trenton rushed over to the scanner. "What makes it special? Stronger? Harder? Breaks through the blockage on the Black Hole? What?"

"The device takes it apart on the seams. Boom. It broke apart fast after we got off, and we only got off because I ordered it. I think they might have been okay with us dying." He smiled. I didn't know why. There was nothing remotely happy about what he was saying. "It transports people faster than any ship can. It makes the ship we're about to find sort of a stationary object. It doesn't need to be a ship per se, except that it has to be able to get to where it's going to begin with."

I looked between them; I didn't understand. "I'm missing this. Can you explain?"

"They can transport troops very fast." Kellan ran a hand through his hair. "It eliminates the need to move ships to get people here. They can build up ships right there next to that one and just move their troops in. Cuts their time to get across the Hole considerably."

Blaze stretched his feet out in front of him. "Cuts it by years. They can be here in days. But it works in both directions. If we can get on that ship and get on the device, we don't have to travel this Hole. We can be there tomorrow."

"THEN IT'S EVEN MORE important we impress upon the leadership that they not do this, not keep coming at us." I walked to the window to look out at nothing. It was something to do. I had to move my body. "If they can get to us so much faster, then it's even more pressing."

Blaze nodded. "I agree. The trouble is that unless they've changed it, we can only move through one at a time. That means we're in an incredible amount of danger until each of us gets through. I'm not worried about me. But now it seems the time to tell you what I hadn't planned on saying until we get there, which is that I have no intention of putting you in danger, Sienna. We need you. I hate to put it like this, but you were absolutely here to bait them. You knew it too. Suggested it more than once. But I had no intention of letting you near danger, despite your strength. You are too important."

I wasn't any more so than any of them, but there it was, that was how they loved me. They all put me first. I nodded. "Nothing you've said surprised me. I don't agree, but I know that's how you feel."

"Right. Now we get on that ship and get to Evander. We're either leaving you here on this ship alone while we travel through the galaxy or we're taking you into danger."

Wade cleared his throat. "Ari said she had to do this. That it had to be her. The estrogen. I know that doesn't mean anything to you guys because you're just seeing the battle, but I keep thinking about it. In what ways is she not the same as you are? How is it different?"

"Wade?" Trenton rocked back on his feet. "Go on."

"I tried to keep her from getting anything but the immunity from the nanos. It didn't work. I thought it was because I was bad at my job. But we followed the model that Ari used when he took out Canyon's eye alterations that were screwing up his brain. He left some in there to help repair. With instructions just to repair. They did that. So why didn't it work for you?"

I didn't know. "I'm sure it's not your fault."

"You're sweet, my love. But it's absolutely my fault and not because I fucked up recoding nanos. I didn't and Cash double-checked my work. He's really good. Did both of us get it wrong?" He put his hands on his hips. "No, we didn't. And nanos aren't so unpredictable that they just do things like that. Unless..."

His voice trailed off, and this time I was actually able to fill in the blanks. "Unless Evander didn't make female Super Soldiers for a reason."

"Exactly." He took my hand in his. "The coding of the nanos that alters the genes, enhances them, it seems to be affected by the estrogen in your system. It is simply doing what it wants to do. They wouldn't like that. Too hard to control. And maybe that is why it had to be you. Why Ari said that it did. Because at the end of it, it's really about you.

Not us. There is something about you that will scare them enough that they will back off our quadrant." He looked at Blaze. "I don't love her any less than you do. I can assure you of that. I'd gladly die for her, too. But we may have to bring her. I have more trust in Ari than you do. If he said it, he meant it. And you guys know Canyon? Would he lie?"

"In a heartbeat," Devil answered for Blaze. "If it kept Waverly and the kids alive. But I don't think they were lying. That's not how they'd have gone about it. If they needed Sienna dead, they'd have come back and killed her. They had ample time to do that."

Anders groaned. He clearly still had a headache. I could see it in the way he lifted his cheekbones slightly. "Of course, then they'd have had to kill all of us because we'd have slaughtered them."

"Then they'd have done it while we slept or knocked us all out. I assure you, Canyon and Rohan were well trained in murder."

Blaze groaned. "Yes, I'm the one who trained them. Better yet, they'd have gotten us all on this ship and blown us up. Let's assume they didn't have murderous intent. Let's assume that Wade is right. We need her. Why not tell us? Hey, we need Sienna because she's a woman to xyz. Why the vagueness?"

"That's not how the time travel messages work." Trenton sighed. "From what little I know, they say just enough so that we fit into certain criteria without fucking it up. Too much information can make things go badly." He threw his hands up in the air. "But I only know bits and pieces of this shit, so I could be totally wrong."

I held up my hand. "I wouldn't be here if I didn't need to do something important."

Just then the ship jolted left. We all fell toward the wall except for Blaze, who was seated. He spun in his chair, and with a total calmness I only associated with him, spoke to us. "Battle stations. The ship I found has found us."

I didn't have anywhere to go in a battle. This was a pretty consistent problem for me during these times, but there was nothing to do about it, so basically my job consisted of getting the heck out of everyone's way. If I followed Wade, he'd have to concern himself with me, too. That left me basically putting myself in my room and sitting tight.

Someday there would have to be something more to do with myself than this.

I ran down the hall and abruptly stopped. In front of me were three men who had not been there before. It was like they were a blur, and then they were on the ship. The machine that Blaze spoke about. It wasn't on our vessel, so how were they suddenly here? That was beyond my understanding. I had finally figured out the lights.

I darted left and jumped over the men just as they noticed me. They stared at each other and then back at me. Okay, they hadn't known I had my abilities, but they did now. I ran.

"They're on the ship," I shouted as loud as I could, knowing that was overkill, but Wade and Trenton couldn't hear as well as we could.

This wasn't like when Kellan chased me. There was nothing exciting about this, it was terrifying. I was strong and capable but totally untrained, and these were men who lived their days and nights to be able to capture someone like me.

"Hey," Corbin called out to them, and they swung around to stare at him. One of them lifted a device I'd never seen before.

In two seconds, Corbin had plowed one into another and grabbed the device. "Fuck, no. You are not taking me out with one of those things again."

Those things? I remembered suddenly about the devices on the planet that had taken down the guys. Some sort of neurological disruption. No, we didn't need that. I rushed over and grabbed the one on the bottom of the pile Corbin made.

"What do we do?"

"Give him to me." Anders rushed down the hall and grabbed the one I held. "You get safe. Where you were with Kellan yesterday. Go there. Now."

I nodded. Fine. Nothing had changed much. The best thing I could do would be to not get caught or in the way. I turned to run again, but two more men stood there. "Guys."

"Fuck." Corbin called out. "Devil, we need you here now."

"Little busy." Whack. Wherever Devil was, he was obviously in a fight.

But I was never without my own ability to save myself. I zapped the two new men, hard. They both hit their knees. A little bit of dizziness overtook me, and I held on to the wall. That wasn't good. I'd zapped harder than I ever had before, and I hadn't rolled with it, like I might have wished. No, it was still a bit of an ordeal.

Corbin was at my side. He gripped my arm, a warm strong presence. "You okay?"

"Give me two seconds and I will be."

He nodded. "Take two. No one is getting near you." Artemis jarred left, and Corbin hit the wall. "Damn it, Blaze, get them away from us."

My dizziness stopped. "Why is Blaze flying and not Trenton?"

"He's shooting," Corbin supplied. "Sienna, listen. This isn't the best time, but..."

Whatever he was going to say, I never got to hear. Two more men appeared. That was interesting. They kept coming in twos. How were they getting here? They ripped Corbin away from me before they pulled out the device. It was loud, deafening, and I no more got to hear Anders shout a warning before it happened. Corbin hit the ground in front of me, and Anders toppled over.

The two who had appeared didn't. They had something in their ears to prevent hearing the noise. I panted from the pain but didn't fall over. The man in front of me was tall— not surprising—and blond. He tilted his head. "How are you upright?"

I didn't know the answer to that, but even if I did, I wasn't going to explain it to this ass. I acted with instinct. The one holding me was distracted from the fact that I was okay, and that meant I got to swing right at his face. I'd never punched anyone before, and it hurt. In fact, I was pretty sure I'd broken my thumb from the wrenching pain that followed, but he doubled over, and I kneed him hard, right in the gut.

Some things, it turned out, were just instinctual.

"How are you doing that?" Strong hands grabbed me.

"I don't know," another new person answered, "but we need to bring her back. They're going to want to see her."

I kicked and scratched. No one would say I didn't try. But there were five of them now and one of me. Corbin and Anders were still not moving, and that sound they'd blasted had probably taken all of the guys down. I couldn't even blame us for getting caught like this. How were they getting on Artemis? If we'd known, I'm sure they would have blocked their ears.

"I'm going to be okay." I didn't know if that were true or if anyone who loved me could even hear me. But I needed to say it just in case.

"Oh no." The man holding me laughed. "You really aren't."

* * *

All Evander ships looked the same. I was convinced of it. Pods. Dead-eyed men wandering around following orders. Smaller leaders with attitudes giving those orders. Metal everywhere. I sighed. Bad things happened when I went into space. I was more and more convinced I had to stay on a planet, barefooted, with the sun on my face. Of course, I'd never been barefooted outside, but that was neither here nor there.

Unlike last time, I wasn't scared. I was fucking annoyed.

My guys were still on Artemis. They weren't dead. I was sure of it. Like me, they were survivors, and if anyone could figure out how to get them all out of this, it was Trenton. That man had an incredible ability to dart and weave. I doubt it had even taken him down.

As if to confirm that, the ship I was on dropped and then shook beneath my feet. Yes, Artemis was firing them on. That meant they were all going to be fine.

But that didn't alter anything at the moment. I was on this ship; they were on Artemis. We were in a black hole, which wasn't normal space. And to get me back, they'd have to disable this ship without killing me. If they even knew I was gone yet.

So much not fun. Plus, whatever the machine was that

was moving them through space so fast made me want to puke. That feeling hadn't ended.

"Mr. Vice President," the asshat holding me said, shoving me forward. "She made it through the device, and she's strangely strong."

Yes, I was. I'd broken his nose. If that made me more than just a little bit happy, that was fine. I didn't have to justify my feelings to anyone. Maybe I was more violent than I realized.

"How is that possible?"

The man in front of me was tiny. Smaller than me. I wasn't used to that with the men around me. They were all huge. I had to look down to speak to him. That didn't mean I judged him for being short. No, it was more the fact that he was that high up in Evander that made me get on my judgmental bandwagon.

Stupid ass...

"I don't know, but I think we should get her home before the competition gets her."

I stared at him. The what? I wasn't going to ask. But that seemed like an important piece of information. By competition, they couldn't mean us. We weren't that.

But then it dawned on me, as cliché as it was, as though a light was going off in my mind. A bell ringing. Evander was a corporation. A business. Even where we were from, we had them. Small versions. If one person selling shoes undercut the cost of shoes, all the stores had to do that.

Who was Evander competing with for sales? They wanted our side of the galaxy for our commodities. One of which was me.

"Oh you don't want to lose me." I smiled. I needed them to think me valuable so that I could be kept alive long enough to either figure out how to save myself or to be rescued. I didn't care which as long as no one I cared about got hurt.

It was amazing, really. I hadn't wanted anyone hurt for me, but my heart had changed on that issue. I didn't care if any of these men here had bad things happen to them. That might sound awful if I said it aloud, but in my thoughts, I was totally comfortable. From this moment, there was us and there was them. If they weren't part of us, they were them. Innocents could be us.

That wasn't these guys.

Fuck. Them.

"What?" The Vice President walked toward us. "Who are you?"

"I'm the woman you guys have been trying to get for some time on the other side of the galaxy. I'm a big get for you."

He blinked. "The one they made sick."

"Yes, they did, but I beat that. I'm amazing. I can do it with my brain." I pointed at my head. "You really don't want to mess with me."

His mouth fell open. "That's not possible. I heard that they dosed you with everything."

I smiled. "They did, but I'm just kind of awesome."

He shook his head. Being an asshole must come as a job requirement for Vice Presidents in this place.

I zapped him. Not even a hard hit, and he fell to his knees, grabbing his head.

"Oh, yes," the one holding me said, a bland tone to his voice. "She can do that, too."

No way had he forgotten that part. It was a pretty substantially strange thing for a person to be able to do. Did he want me to zap the Vice President?

He had no idea how much worse I could do to all of

them. I stared at my wrist. It still read zero. But would it if I opened myself to taking their emotions? Could my body continue to hold the virus at bay and do that? Could I trust myself that far?

What would Wade say if he was standing here?

That was sort of obvious. He'd say stay alive, Sienna. Wait for us to save you. We're coming. Don't be stupid. Don't do that again. Something along those lines.

The Vice President stumbled to his feet. He looked a little bit like a rag doll, like he couldn't make the bones in his legs work. How hard had I zapped him? I'd been going for easy. I had no resulting dizziness, so it couldn't have been that bad. Maybe he was just... not strong.

I didn't know, didn't care. What I wanted was to get out of here and fast. They had to stop firing on Artemis. She held everyone I loved in the universe in her strong structure. I wasn't going to lose any of them.

"Stop firing on Artemis, or I'll zap you again." I leaned forward. "Harder."

His voice cracked when he finally found it. "Stop firing."

I turned slightly to the Super Soldier holding me. "I love the men on that ship. They're Super Soldiers, like you. They have a life. They have me. You can have it, too. So just know that there is more than this. You don't have to listen to this man."

The Vice President's eyes widened. I let myself listen to his heart. There were incredible benefits to this ability. He was terrified. His heart raced much faster than it should. If I cared if he lived or died, I would actually be worried about this.

But I didn't.

He was afraid. Of me. I smiled, slowly. "You don't need

to mess with Artemis anymore. I'm the most interesting thing you were going to find there."

"We know that ship. Every time we find that ship, whoever is on it causes us endless problems." His chin shook.

I leaned forward as far as I could. "Stop firing on my ship, or next time I'll make it hurt."

"Stop firing," he practically shouted. "Stop."

I could have laughed. Every person on this ship, including me, could have heard him if he whispered, and he had to shout to get what he needed done. That was pathetic. Real leadership shouldn't need this. The Super Soldiers here didn't respect him, they tolerated him. That meant it would be pretty easy to take off his head. If I wanted that to happen.

I didn't. I just wanted them to leave me alone.

"We... we can't let this woman on our ship." The man hollered again. "She's going to turn your head. Make you all want to fuck her."

I blinked at him. Okay. Now that had come from left field. I hadn't considered that. There were risks with the fact that many of these people had maybe never seen a woman before. But then again, they were put in machines that chemically castrated them every so often so they wouldn't have those urges. I hadn't met the five Super Soldiers I loved until they'd worked through much of this.

Did the Vice President want to scare me? It wouldn't work. I straightened my back. "I don't believe that anyone on this ship would be so awful. Don't you have control of your men?"

He grabbed my arm. "If you zap me again, I will have them beat you. They do what I say."

I looked over my shoulder at the man with the broken

nose. "Are you going to beat me? You didn't even lift a finger to hurt me when I broke your nose. You aren't. He's a liar, and you could kill him and don't. What does that tell me? You're gentle inside. I don't even know your name and I know that."

The Vice President hauled me away from the man who'd held me. How far did I want to let this go? Once I showed my cards to this man, I couldn't undo that. But the fact remained, if I could get my arm back from Devil and Blaze, I could easily subdue the Vice President of the moment and his pathetic attempts at manipulation.

I'd managed to get him to stop firing on Artemis, that bought me some time. Should I just...

He dug his fingers into my arm, and the answer came instinctually. I yanked my arm back, shoving the ass into the side of the wall in the process.

Well... that solved that. I put my hands on my hips. "Don't touch me like that again. I'm strong and tough. I never knew that, not my whole life, but I do now, and I'm done with this bullshit."

"I'm done with it, too. Trance, grab her."

Stronger hands held me from behind, his arms gentler but tougher on my upper arms. This was a harder hold to get out of, and I didn't know. We were supposed to have years on Artemis. I'd only advanced to jump higher. I'm sure if Kellan had known we had such a brief training period, he'd have gotten to this part faster.

Instinct could only get me so far.

"Put her in the Carrier. Let them deal with her at home. I have a job. I intend to do it. I don't want a woman here."

The Carrier? It had to be the...

I never got to finish that thought as I was stuck in a chair, strapped in, and the door closed around me.

"Hey," I yelled out. It was pitch black, and this couldn't be good news. I bit down on my lip, knowing my time to deal with this was coming to an end. "You don't have to do this."

The pitch blackness changed to bright lights.

"Someone came back through, Johnny," a voice called out, and I blinked through the haze that assaulted my head. That had been awful, like a sped up yet longer version of whatever they'd been doing to get from Artemis to their Evander ship and back. I grabbed my head. They'd sent me somewhere.

The door flung open, and two men—of the non-Super Soldier variety—stared at me. They were medium-sized, dark-haired—they might even be brothers, they looked so much alike—and they wore matching uniforms. Gray with the letter *E* in the corner.

Okay. That settled it. I was at Evander. Probably their headquarters.

"It's a girl, Johnny." The one not named Johnny stated the obvious while Johnny shook his head, silent so far.

I had a number of choices. They'd thrown me through this capsule-thingy. I had to use that for my benefit. What did that mean? Punch these guys out? Probably not. That would only take me so far. I wasn't a Super Soldier, that was abundantly obvious, and they'd catch me. If I started hostile, I'd get hostile back.

With no idea how many people were in this facility, I certainly wasn't going to take now to test my emotion-taking ability. That wouldn't get me anywhere. I had to get back to the guys, but the only way currently to do that was back through the machine that brought me here and into the hands of that Vice President I should have just killed.

But there was the whole I-wasn't-sure-I-had-the-stomach-for-it problem.

And these two might not deserve the killing. They might be an us and not a them.

I was overthinking things, and I had to make a decision. So I made one that occurred to me on the spot. I dropped to my knees. "Oh, please help me, kind sirs." It was enough to make me gag, but I was doing it. For now, let them think I was a damsel in distress because I sort of was. "Help me. Things are so bad in that place. That man, the Vice President, he threatened and threatened me."

Johnny finally spoke. "Oh, miss. Yes, you're a girl. Sorry, we've never seen one before." I couldn't imagine that. We didn't have very many women on our side of the galaxy. A virus had wiped out most of the women, and a substantial amount more boys were born than girls. However, we did have enough that most people would have at least seen a woman in their lives. What were they doing with them over here?

I answered my own unasked question: they hid them away like chattel. There was some of that where I was from, too. Just not on my own planet. I'd been luckier than I knew. It hadn't been perfect, but it had been a lot better than most places. Sometimes the grass is greener at home.

"We'd better take her to the executives," Not-Johnny

spoke again. "We can't have her here. There's no one sched-
uled to go through today. Unsanctioned use will be a problem. And... and I'm not getting blamed for this."

I watched through lowered eyes. The perfect blend, I
hoped, of scared and needy. In the meantime, I listened. No
one else was coming through today. That didn't mean that
they couldn't have someone come through like I just did.
Someone to follow me and give me away. If I were the Vice
President over there, that's what I'd do. I chewed on my lip.
How should I try to make the next moments happen? What
did they need to be?

"You know they're not going to be happy while they're
in negotiations with Faustas Corporation."

Now that caught my attention. I kept my eyes down.
"Sorry? I'm so confused. Who are these people you're
discussing?"

"She must be from through that black hole. Can you
imagine? We have a girl here, and she doesn't know any of
this. Not Evander, Johnny. Not Faustas and the proposed
takeover of all their property. This girl knows nothing."

Oh this woman knew quite a lot now. It was everything
I could do not to smile. I might not know how to work the
lights, but I understood humans well enough and the basics
of Evander. They had another corporation here that they
had to do business with.

Maybe I could screw that up. Mess it up enough that
Evander stopped coming through the galaxy to destroy our
lives. I was supposed to be the one to do it, and I knew it
wasn't going to be because I went on a killing rampage that I
wasn't cut out to do.

Not to mention board members could be replaced. That
happened all the time at the temple. One set of people
would change out, and another would come in to run things.

I could kill people, but unless I was going to become some phantom serial killer of board members, that wasn't going to hold up very well.

I had to do better than that.

I had to be me about it.

I wasn't Melissa, who had gone through the black hole when it took seven years to do it, lived on an ice planet and survived near nuclear destruction. I wasn't Diana, who had crash-landed on this side of the galaxy and made her way back home to run a war base and raise children at the same time. I wasn't Paloma, who I hardly knew, but who had somehow managed to survive being married to the Sandlers during a war with their father and had come out unscathed. I wasn't Waverly with her kind, gentle goodness and amazing ability to travel time and space, and care for others as a nurse. I wasn't Amber with her genius and how she was working as a doctor when women didn't do this.

But I was me. I was the one they'd sent here to do this, and so help me, I was going to get this done.

I was a commodity. I had nanos in me, and I'd fought back every virus Evander put in me with the technological help. I bet there were lots of ways that Faustas could use me to not have to be acquired by Evander.

"Oh, yes," I smiled. "Please take me to whoever is in charge."

This was my time to save the people I loved. Failure was not an option.

* * *

Blaze

. . .

My ears rang, and I shook my head for the hundredth time, hoping it would clear them. That fucking device. We had to acquire it and figure out how our enemies used it and managed to keep their people from falling over from it. But that was a struggle for another day.

They had my girl. She belonged to us, and I'd be damned if they got to keep her a second longer than necessary. She was brave. Shouting how she was fine. Where did she keep finding that inner strength? Who would think to do that when an enemy was kidnapping them? I trained seven-foot men with less courage in their whole body than she had in her pinkie.

"Is it fixed?" I didn't want to pressure Anders, but he had to work faster. Yes, he'd been barely conscious five minutes earlier, but that had been all of us. I didn't know why they'd stopped firing on us, but I wasn't going to hold to the idea that was going to keep going. They'd probably start again any second.

Trenton scooted out from beneath the console with a tool in both hands and a light in his mouth, illuminating the devices for him. Had to be hard to be human sometimes. He couldn't see as well in the dark, and we were going lightless right now. Just barely enough so that humans wouldn't smack into each other.

From the control room, Anders answered me. "Working on it."

Fuck this fucking shit. Okay. I had to breathe. She was okay. Too valuable for them to kill. If I kept saying that, I would believe it. We'd be dead if not for Trenton. He'd had the wherewithal to rip the time device out of the engine. It left us drifting in space but stopped them from being able to zap over here. Yeah... they'd updated the device.

"Thanks for saving us." I spoke to Trenton, but it took him a second too long to answer me.

He blinked. "Don't thank me. I didn't get it done fast enough to save her."

That was true for all of us. I squatted in front of him. "You okay?"

I checked his sounds. Heart was strong. But he was in pain. I could hear it in the clench of his jaw. The starts and stops of his breathing.

Trenton nodded. That hurt him too. "I'm fine."

I could argue with him. He'd obviously hit his head, and with this crew, he wasn't going to fool us. But we needed him, and if he said he was okay, then I was going to pretend he was until I couldn't anymore. I needed Trenton. He wasn't one of us and yet he was. Maybe he hadn't been made in a vial, shaped with genetic material to better be susceptible to nanos altering him, but he'd been forged in pain and fire. We understood each other. And now that I loved Sienna more than I did breath, my admiration for the fact that he'd somehow withstood grief to take revenge on those who took his wife grew immensely.

If she died, I was done. When I'd woken up from cryo to Waverly's voice, it was as though I'd been pulled to the other side of the galaxy, through the black hole by an unknown tug telling me I had a path to follow. Then I couldn't figure out what that was. It had seemed like I might have made a terrible error and dragged all of these guys with me.

But then she had been—unconscious in the awful cryo state—and I'd known. I had to take care of that blonde angel in the pod. She needed me. That scared the shit out of me. I tried to get rid of her when she first woke up because I don't know how to do fear. I've never been scared in my life.

When you're born with the purpose of dying in battle, to do so is actually to complete one's role in life.

For the first time, I wanted something else.

And fuck me, I still did.

"Anders?" I spoke through gritted teeth.

"Working on it."

I knew he was, but this was taking forever. I looked down at the tablet. Okay, not a full minute had passed. Maybe I was being unreasonable. I took a long breath, and it didn't help. I might actually explode.

The door opened, and Devil strode in. He was covered in blood.

"None of it is mine."

That was good. "Did you—?"

"I took off their heads," he interrupted me, and I didn't even care. Let him. Cut me off. Whatever. Devil was incredibly useful to have around. Kellan would gladly decapitate people, but half the time, I needed him to make the engines run better. It was great to have Devil so readily available to dispatch our enemies without blinking. We were all lethal. He was even more so.

I nodded. "Good." I couldn't take it anymore. "Very useful to have you. Glad you showed up when you did. Wouldn't have ever believed that, but I am."

"Thanks." He smirked. "I'm mildly amused by all of you."

That shouldn't have been funny. Until Sienna was back, every minute had to be deadly serious. Only, it kind of was.

Corbin ran into the room. "I'm taking a shuttle and going to get her."

I blinked. That was unexpected. I wouldn't have thought it from him. He was the one who usually made sure the rest of us got done what had to finish so that we could charge forward. He was as lethal as the rest of us but more valuable in some ways. Corbin didn't forget the things we needed to survive. Like loading food on to the ship.

"Really?"

"Yes." He turned and ran. Devil met my gaze and rushed after him. If Corbin was going, then Devil was, too. I sat down in my chair. Another minute had passed. Damn it.

"Anders?"

"Stop bothering me." The response sounded rightly annoyed. This wasn't me. I wasn't the man who couldn't wait an appropriate time for a rushed job to get done.

Wade ran into the room. "Put this in your ears. It'll stop that blast."

Now that was some good news. "Fuck, Corbin and Devil went after her."

Wade paled. "Tell them to hold off. I'm coming. Tell them." He turned to run after them. Everyone had something to do, somewhere to go. For me, I had to make sure it all got done. Rushing forward, going first—that hadn't been me since I'd taken command. And I'd never felt less in control of anything in my life than I did right then.

* * *

Sienna

They put me in an office and went to get help. Okay. Here I was. Now what? I'd managed to hide the fact that, for now, I was strong and full of nanos that were keeping me that way. I stared down at my arm. It still read zero. Maybe there would be a time I could count on that, but I wasn't there mentally yet.

Through the thin wall, I could hear people talking. What they said was muffled, but this area had thin enough walls that I could make out the sound of annoyance. Whoever was talking to each other in there, they weren't happy.

I whirled around. What on Earth did I think I would find in this office? I had no idea. What did people put in their offices? Was this one even active or just an empty place Johnny and Not-Johnny put me in?

I wasn't going to stand here and wait to be caught by someone who actually knew what was going on. I didn't know what the men who had found me did, but I didn't get the feeling that they were very high up in this organization. I'd place credits on the idea that the higher executives had seen women. Also, if they'd known much of anything, they'd know that the Super Soldiers were castrated to the point that they wouldn't have been a threat to me. At least not sexually.

None of that mattered. I had to concentrate, and that was easier said than done. I was tough. I was tough. Maybe if I said it enough, I'd believe it. There was a building full of people here who could hear my heartbeat and tell things about me that even I didn't know how to do yet.

I swallowed and steeled my back. There hadn't been people when they'd brought me to this room outside. If I was lucky, maybe there still wasn't.

I rushed through the door. It wasn't locked. I almost felt bad for Not-Johnny who hadn't latched it. But his loss was my gain in this case.

The space I came out into was a big open room filled with desks and lots of machines I couldn't identify. That was okay. I could use the lights. The thought brought up Corbin, which really made me grin. It was like he was with me, showing me how to do basic things.

Whoever was in the other room continued to shout. They were really not happy. But now I could hear the words. Deal. Negotiation. Losing. They hated Evander. My heart sped up, and I tried to force it to calm. I bet it was someone from that other company yelling.

Could I really do this? Yes, I could. I was going to stop Evander. They'd never see me coming. I opened that door and walked in.

* * *

Devil

I broke the neck of the next one who came at me. Those fuckers had tried to board our shuttle. No one boarded my shuttle if I didn't want them to. This was my ship, my people, and they were going to give me back my girl. They'd tried to use that device again, but our doctor was as good as theirs. Probably better, although Wade had no fucking confidence. We'd work on that. After we got back Sienna and eliminated these threats.

That's all they were. A temporary setback in what would otherwise be a wonderfully completed mission. I could always tell when things were going well and when they weren't. This was an all-go finale. I felt it in my bones. Just like I'd woken up knowing the day I would be taken prisoner by Sterling and the others who delivered me to Chen would be a loss. My first *L* in years. But it turned out to be a big one and the best L to ever happen to me. Yes, it brought me to Sienna. Taught me to be human.

I hadn't known I wanted to be that.

But I did. Badly. First, because it had seemed the thing to do to get out of my situation in prison and then after for her. I wanted to be the kind of man she could love.

And somehow—fuck—she had.

Now, however, I had to be my old self. I had to end everyone here until I got to Sienna.

"I can't hear her." Corbin spoke, and it jarred my attention. I hadn't been listening, I'd been too busy ending.

My stomach tightened and fear, an emotion I never had time for, struck me silent. It was almost hard to speak. "Is she dead?"

"I don't know." Corbin stormed forward. "But I'm going to find out."

I should have known she'd be dead. I'd done too many bad things in the universe to have something as beautiful as Sienna. I was never going to get to keep her. The Chens had taught me about energy, that it could be moved, manipulated, heard. It was about frequency, but they had a spiritual edge to them that was impossible to deny. What you put out, you got back. And Sienna had just died because I was such a bad fucking person.

I was taking all of these sheep with me. Every one of them would know pain before they died because...

"She's not dead." Corbin held an executive in a choke hold. It was a lethal maneuver. Sometimes you could keep them alive, but that was clearly not his intention. I looked around. There were dead bodies on the floor all around me.

Wade stared at me for a long second. "Were you even conscious when you did that?"

"Not sure." I shrugged. "If they hurt a hair on her head, that was better than they deserved."

Wade smiled at me, a slow one that spoke of pain. "Agreed."

He wasn't like any doctor I'd ever known. But then he'd had pain at the hands of these turds, too. They'd taken him, held him hostage, abused him. Wade was as dark as the rest of us. She brought out the only light we had.

"Where is she?" Because I couldn't hear her, and unless they had wrapped her in one of the devices that hid her, then she wasn't here.

"He put her in the machine Blaze talked about." Corbin dropped the now dead body onto the floor. "He sent her to Evander."

I'd been so lost to all of this that I hadn't even heard that conversation. Talk about a blackout state. This was a new phenomenon for me. Maybe I had to be careful how many people I killed in the future. Oh well, I'd deal with that later.

I grabbed the communicator. Time to tell Blaze what was happening. "Hey, it's me."

"Got her?" Blaze answered, and I shook my head. I'd have answered the same way.

"No, it seems that—"

"Hey." Wade ran forward, but it was too late. Corbin had stuck himself inside of the machine. In seconds, it had gone from off to on, and with a loud boom, Corbin was gone.

I laughed. "Well, it seems that Evander has her now thanks to that machine. But Corbin went after her, and that was that."

"Damn it. No, Kellan, I need you here. Can you go, too? You and Wade?"

I was glad he didn't try to stop me. I'd have done it without his permission, a la Corbin, and then we'd have had a problem. "Sure."

"Good. We're going to fix up Artemis, and I'm sending Trenton over there to see if there is anything we can use. By the time you get back, I want to be back on Artemis, assessing things and away from this mess."

I clicked the button. That sounded like a plan. But Blaze and I both knew that plans went to hell. A lot. The universe was expendable. Everyone but Sienna. I was starting to love these guys like brothers, but I was sure they'd sacrifice me for her. I'd do the same. And while I'd have some regret, I'd do it anyway.

She. Was. Everything.

* * *

Sienna

They stared at me like I had two heads as I plowed through the door. Three men in their fifties. One of them stumbled to his feet. "Miss? Can we help you?"

Women really were like mythical creatures here. None of them knew what to do when they saw me. "My name is Sienna MacKinnon. And I'm here to save you in your negotiations. I'm really special, and if you use the things I can give you, they can't touch you in the marketplace." I hoped that was what it was called. "I can make you more money than you ever imagined."

They stared at each other and finally the one seated all the way to the left rose. "Are you lying? Is this some kind of trick?"

"No, but we're in a building filled with Super Soldiers. So I'm here to tell you we don't have time. Do you have a syringe? You're going to want to take my blood."

The first one who spoke shook his head. "No, we're just the deal makers. We don't carry that."

"Well, then I'm going to suggest that one of you run out there and find one. I wouldn't know where to look. My blood is key. I am a Super Soldier, basically. I have all the makings of one in me. Something they don't let happen. If you want to compete with them, I'm going to need you to take my blood and, uh, sign an agreement to leave my people alone. Always."

The silent one ran from the room. "This will drop their stocks right? And raise yours?"

Nods followed my questions. "Why are you doing this?" Lefty asked me. "Why help us?"

"At this point, I don't care who is good and who is bad. I know Evander is coming after my people. I don't want them invading our space anymore. If you prove to be a problem, I can assure you that I have a lot of people on my side who can blow you to smithereens. You won't like that."

He smiled, slowly. "You know why they don't make women, right? It's because it takes care of the fertility problem. We've seen the science. They won't show anyone how to do it because the same tech, the manipulation of the female system, it could end our girl problem. What you're giving us, it could take away the power to control love and reproduction. You might just save the universe." He took off his glasses. "Oh, and we'll be richer than any of us could imagine."

It really did always come down to that. But that was fine. If I could help anyone have a full life, then this would be worth it beyond my own needs. I had to stop Evander.

"Once you get my blood, I'm going to suggest you run. I have no idea how long we'll get to be okay before the wrong person hears repeated to them what we just said."

This was why Ari and Canyon had sent me here. It wasn't just us. We really could save everyone.

But what happened to me now? I had no idea.

Corbin

I forced the door to the transport machine open and stepped out of it, knowing immediately where I was. I'd lived here, mostly in the basement, for several years when I'd gotten out of training. That was when they'd made me a killer. Before that, my job had sometimes required death dealing, but here is where they made it so I didn't care.

Sure, these days I'd tamed. I'd done it the second I'd met Sienna. I'd grown my hair out for years, done things that made me seem loose and easy, but it wasn't until I met her that I meant it. She was my everything. Evander had been my reason for living for a long time. They'd made me, literally, and I owed them my existence. Now? That was all Sienna. Her existence had remade me.

I listened for her heartbeat, and it met my ears, fast, as though the sounds of her living homed me in instantly. Good, now I'd find her.

"Hey," someone called, and I looked over my shoulder

at them. It was a small man, maintenance crew. They liked to bully us around here because we were relatively sedated when we were in this building. I was fairly certain that was because they'd drugged us to keep us tame here. And then when those drugs wore off, we'd be even more lethal. But that didn't matter now because he thought I was one of the ones that worked here, and didn't know that I didn't currently have an ounce of restraint in my body when it came to not ending his life.

This whole building could burn once Sienna was out of it.

"Why were you touching that?"

I looked where the man indicated. He must be in charge of this thing, guarding it or something. They probably never gave any thought to non-Evander people coming through it. Why would they? Who in the hell would want to come here if they didn't have to?

"I'm not touching it." I stated the obvious. This guy had about ten more seconds of my time before he was done.

"I saw you touching it, and what is with your hair? Why did they let you grow it like that?"

I sighed. Done. Done. Done. I grabbed him, and his eyes widened before I threw him against the side of the wall. He went down, not dead but unconscious. If he woke up, he'd report this, but my guess would be that by then, they'd know I was here.

Following Sienna's heartbeat, I ran.

She was three floors above me, that meant the offices. That's where the executives were. I spent one whole day there following a douchebag around while he showed me off as some model to his superiors that they should invest in. It really always came down to money.

There were five ways to get there. The stairs would be

the fastest, and no one ever used them. I sped toward them as fast as I was able to run.

I wasn't going to lose Sienna before I had a chance to really show her how much I loved her. As usual, I'd hesitated too long, waited because I had no idea what I was doing with regular human relationships. For the first time in my life, I'd been afraid. I had to get her back to undo that. To explain. She was my love. She had to know.

* * *

Sienna

"We don't have to run with it." The man to the left spoke fast.

I rubbed my arm where he'd just taken my blood. I pressed a tissue to it, but it was already clotting. The benefit of my nanos. I healed fast. "Why not?"

The door flung open, and two panting executives stood there. "What are you doing?" One of them charged at us, and I zapped him, sending him backward into the wall. The other one abruptly stopped.

"Because it's in the tablet and sent to our people. Mr. Wordwith, we take back our offer. We don't need to be acquired by you. We are now on our way to leaving. And we'll be taking Miss..." His voice trailed off. "I can't remember your name, and you just saved our whole company."

I smiled at him and then the executives who came in. "My name is Sienna, and you have been fucking with my life. I've had enough of it."

One of them stumbled up from the wall he'd hit when I zapped him. They stared at each other. "Do you know anything about messing with a Sienna?"

The other one stayed so quiet that I knew that he did. His heart rate kicked up. I walked toward him. "You do, don't you?" I zapped him, just a smidge, and he yelped before his eyes widened. "You know how you made me sick and then tried to have me kidnapped again and again?" I threw my arms in the air. "Hurt countless numbers of people. Scared me. Threatened those I loved? Well, here I am, but guess what, I'm not sick, and I'm stronger than I've ever been." Rage surged through me. It was an unusual feeling from me. But maybe I'd just had enough. The thing about rage, I quickly realized, was that it didn't respond to logic. Yes, I knew this was a bad idea. I had no one to help me if this went wrong.

But I wanted to hurt them. I spent so much time not doing that, on making sure everyone else was fine. On trying not to be such a burden to everyone around me, to make sure I left no negative footprints anywhere I went, that I was simply done from the effort. At least one of these fuckers had known what was happening to me. Maybe he had ordered it.

"We needed to understand how you do what you do. We can't have others with that power. It would change the corporate balance of power. It would lower our stock prices."

I pretended to wipe away a tear. "You're about to have a bad day. Your stock prices will be the last thing you have to worry about, ever. In fact, you may never feel anything again."

I opened up my abilities. I was going to suck this asshole dry. There was a change in me. It used to be sort of out of control for me to do this, but now it was easy. I could take everything out of him, and he'd be dead. I was clear about that.

The door flung open. I hardly noticed. If they wanted to hurt me, I'd deal with them, too. Someone picked up the man I was about to emotionally lobotomize, and he snapped his neck before he dropped him to the floor.

"I thought we told you that we'd do the killing."

I sucked back my power. "Corbin?" My voice shook. "How are you here?"

He put his arms around me. "Kellan isn't the only one who will always find you." He shot daggers to the others in the room. "Anyone else need to die?"

I let him hold me, my body vibrating slightly. I couldn't say why. "No. I mean, a lot of people probably do, but that one was responsible."

He nodded once. "Fine."

"We'll take care of them. And here." The man I'd just made very wealthy handed me the paper I'd made them fill out. "We won't ever come to your side of the galaxy. I can say that for sure, but I've also put it in writing. This is my company. I'm Max Faustas. We're not interested in doing anything but getting out from under Evander's thumb here."

The door flung open again. This time it was Devil. How had they all gotten here? A second later, Wade appeared. They were both panting.

"There is a huge crew of Soldiers heading in. Are you listening to this?"

I hadn't been. But I opened my ears. Yes, there was a lot of chatter, a lot of yelling. We were in a lot of trouble.

"What do we do?"

Devil stared at the executives across the desk. "Despite what they said, I'm going to suggest they run. They're good at getting people killed. Do it. Now. While we're still here to distract them. And whatever she gave you that is going to let you win? Do it fast. Or else we'll come back, and you won't like what happens when we do."

Did he really intend to come back to this side of the galaxy, or were we stuck here? Corbin tugged my hand. "As for us, we're going to run."

Wade groaned. "There are a ton of them between us and where we need to go."

"Right," Devil said. "So you keep Sienna alive and leave what is between us and transportation out of here to Corbin and me?"

Wade nodded once. "I promise."

I almost argued. At this point I didn't need anyone to keep me alive. I was pretty darn capable of handling it. But I wasn't going to argue. They were right. I'd never killed anyone. I was about to, but Corbin had stopped that.

If I tried to interfere, I might make this worse.

Corbin and Devil fought through lines of men as though they'd been doing it together for years. That wasn't true. In fact, they'd only been on a permanent same team for a brief period of time with me. For a number of years, they'd been enemies. But they were almost beautiful. Wade grabbed my arm, yanking me backward. I was going to have to speak to him about what had happened to me with my rage, but I wasn't going to do that right now.

We might need that rage. Seeing Corbin had deflated it, but it was still there, in the back of my head. A thought dawned on me. What if it wasn't my own that I was feeling?

What was amazing about the constant killing I saw in front of me was that they were fighting men who were as trained as they were. I'd no sooner thought that than a whole additional crowd showed up. My guys were surrounded.

I rushed forward, and Wade yanked me back, surprisingly strongly. I could have gotten away, but his tug reminded me that I didn't want to make this worse.

"Wade, we have to do something."

He smiled. "No, we don't."

How could he think that? Why was he smiling? That was when I saw them. Blaze. Kellan. Anders. Trenton. How and when had they gotten here? The lights flashed dark. Most of us could still see, but I was sure Trenton had just suddenly done that because it was, at least for the half a second it mattered, totally distracting.

My guys pounced. And then they pounded.

"Sienna," Trenton called. "Wade. This way."

I ran toward him. What did he want us to do? He didn't tell me, but it wasn't the time. I ran after him, and it was soon obvious to me that we were heading back to the machine. But we couldn't go without the others.

"Trenton?"

He shook his head. "We can only send two through at a time anyway. You and Wade. Then me. The others will make it. I trust them. That's all this takes. We have to trust each other. They'll get through. They're not leaving you. I promise you that. Neither am I."

On the ground, Not-Johnny groaned. Why was he doing that? I didn't have time to ask. I stepped in the device.

There was darkness. And then light.

* * *

Wade

"You okay?" I pulled Sienna out of the machine. She put her hands on her knees like she had to catch her breath, and

I wished I had anything to scan her with. When I'd darted after Devil and Corbin, I hadn't been exactly prepared to battle.

I kissed her cheek. "Sienna?"

"What if I did everything wrong? What if the guys aren't coming back? What if everyone gets killed?"

I squatted down in front of her. There were just some things I had to say, that I had to make her hear. "Sienna, maybe whatever you did will turn out to be a mistake. Maybe it won't. We can't predict the future. I don't care what our time travelers say. They don't really know. They do some kind of thing to get us to behave in ways we hope are the right ways, but really, screw it. No one really knows, Sienna. We're all doing the best we can."

That was good and fine until I really stopped to examine it. "But what if I made something worse?"

"Sweetheart, you didn't cause any of this mess. I'm not sure what you did, but I can't believe you could make it worse."

I swallowed. "Wade, I gave my blood to a competing corporation. They think they can fix the fertility issue."

He blinked. "Really?"

I realized my mistake almost as soon as I said the words. Wade wasn't going to be particularly concerned with the corporate part now. He stared at me. "Did they think they could do that? Based on your blood?"

"The nanos and whatever. The Super Soldier alterations in females has something to do with the fertility issue. The girl babies."

He took me in his arms and pulled me to him. "Well, then let them fix that here. And we can fix it back at home."

Really? "Wade, what if it doesn't stop the Evander problem?"

"Well, then let's let someone else solve the Evander problem. You're a walking miracle. You're going to save everyone."

The machine made a noise, and a second later Corbin and Trenton stepped through it. Corbin groaned. "I hate that fucking thing."

Trenton smiled. "I've been through worse things. Don't worry, honey, they're all coming back. We're actually going to get out of this."

Wade squeezed me tighter. "We're going to do better than get out of it."

I hoped he was right.

* * *

Sienna

From my window on Artemis, I watched them blow the Evander ship to smithereens. They hadn't tried to follow us through the machine back to the ship. All that technology and they hadn't wanted to try to protect it?

I heard Corbin approach my room before he entered it. Their heartbeats were officially distinct to me. Like the way I could sometimes tell by the way someone sounded walking who they were, I could hear their heartbeats that way now, too. He didn't say a word, and I didn't turn from where I watched the burning Evander ship.

His arms came around me a second before his mouth touched my neck, planting a kiss. I shuddered. That was so nice it almost distracted me from what was happening. "Why would they let us go? Let that ship get blown up with their expensive travel machine on it?"

Corbin kissed me again. He smelled clean like he just showered. "Because they have a serious problem now. You let their intellectual property get away from them. They could lose everything. At the end of the day, they only used war to increase profit. It's not the same as the Sandler battles or anyone else. They don't care about us now. Not with a chairman of the board to fire and other issues to handle. My guess would be that you did it."

"What will happen to all those Super Soldiers?"

He turned me in his arms, and I ran my hands over his shirt, feeling his strong muscles beneath my hands. "If Evander falls apart, they'll have to make a life somewhere. Again, you aren't responsible for the universe. You did what you could do, and I'm proud of you. Besides, isn't it enough you may be the key to saving humanity's fertility issue?"

I shrugged. "I didn't really do that. I just survived the nanos."

He lifted me up, and I wrapped my arms around his waist. He swung me around but didn't set me down anywhere, instead keeping me tightly wound around him. "Sometimes the best we can do is live another day." Corbin kissed my chin. "I love you."

Sweet man. He was the one who had taught me things when I first woke up on this ship. Corbin was kind to a fault. Even if he didn't know it. I kissed him hard. "Why didn't you come to me before now? Playing hard to get?"

I couldn't imagine I was dealing with the same thing I'd had with Kellan. He wasn't playing some kind of game. Corbin shook his head. "I've never done this before. The longer it went on, the more I was afraid I'd be a disappointment. The others seemed to know what they were doing or how to fake confidence on this better. I got scared I'd let you down."

In a million years, I'd never have imagined him saying that to me. "Corbin, let's lie down together. You couldn't have let me down. Ever. I'm hardly some kind of sex judge, and I want to be with you. It's just the two of us in here, not everyone else, and it's not a comparison game."

He nodded and did as I asked. We lay in the bed fully dressed for a long second regarding each other. I ran my hand down the slope of his nose. He really was so beautiful. "Kiss me."

Corbin nodded, and I lost myself when his mouth met mine. He'd taken care of me, I was going to take care of his heart, always.

He made love to my mouth. Funny he'd been nervous because he quickly got over that and fast. Corbin traveled his hands under my shirt and pinched my nipples. I giggled. There was something a little bit forbidden about the way we were doing this. As though staying fully clothed, even though we touched each other, meant we might suddenly stop if someone walked in. Of course, no one was going to do that, but I liked the forbidden just the same.

I reached under his clothes and stroked his cock in his pants. It was difficult. He was hard and his pants were tight, but still I managed. He liked it, or at least I assumed he did from the moans, which increased in volume the more that we did this.

I stroked and stroked until he reached out to stop me. "I'll come any second, and I want to be inside of you. That's what I'm thinking about all the time. Obsessively imagining. Is that okay?"

"Of course it's okay, it's more than okay." But I needed something from him first. I wiggled out of my clothes, and he quickly disrobed himself. I took his hand and pressed his fingers inside of me.

He widened his eyes. "I imagined you'd be warm, but this is so much better."

"Right there. That's a spot I really like. Could you rub it for a few moments?"

He scooted closer. "Anything you want, always."

Corbin was a fast learner, and that didn't surprise me at all. I soon writhed against him as pleasure traveled through my body. This was exactly what I needed. "Yes, more."

He listened, pressing slightly harder, but I wasn't ready to come. Like Corbin, I needed more, I had to have the connection of his cock in me. It had been too long that we'd not done it. Maybe I just had to have the completion.

"Come inside of me. If you can. Please. Now."

He rolled on top of me. In his gaze was the Corbin I was used to seeing—he was loaded with confidence. I smiled, and he pushed inside of me, inch by inch until he'd filled me up. He closed his eyes.

"Sienna."

I touched his cheek. "I know, Corbin. I'm right there with you."

Together we moved until we had a rhythm that had me writhing beneath him. I couldn't get enough. If this could last forever, it wouldn't be long enough. And yet I needed it to end because what I wanted more than anything was to have his cum deep inside of me, proving he had been there and he was mine.

I wanted to drip with it.

Minutes passed. I dug my fingernails into his back, knowing I wouldn't come until he did. I needed his orgasm to trigger my own. There was too much tension, too much had happened. I had to see Corbin come. That was a must-do for me to find my own. We were in this together.

Finally, he jerked, the sound coming out of his mouth almost painful before it changed into a sigh. Was there ever anything as beautiful as Corbin finding pleasure in my body? I couldn't think of a single thing.

I followed him happily into oblivion.

He kissed my shoulder. "Can we do it again?"

I giggled. "Yep."

This was happiness.

* * *

We pushed Artemis back out of the black hole. She wasn't holding up particularly well, and I was glad we were able to get her out at all, considering that I wasn't sure how we'd get home if she didn't bring us there. Would we have been stuck forever in the black hole? I pushed away that thought. Too many things could go wrong. It was better to simply focus on what did and not obsess about what didn't.

That was harder for me than it should have been.

I walked up behind Wade and Blaze where they watched the screen. "Guys, I had a weird thing happen on Evander."

Wade turned to me and smirked. "Just one?" I elbowed him, and he shook his head. "Sorry, go ahead."

"When I got all angry and rageful, it was like I was channeling an emotion that wasn't my own. It was like I could use someone else's. That's weird, right?"

Blaze turned to me, his brow furrowed. "You store the emotions you take. So it doesn't surprise me that somewhere in that exceptional brain of yours is the excess." He picked up my wrist and looked down at it before he laid a kiss right there. "Still at zero. Whatever you were doing, you're still healthy. We can figure the rest of it out now. I think we'll have a lifetime to do so."

That as the first time any of them had said that. The

idea that it was over, that there were things to do now. I smiled.

"Yes, I guess we have a lifetime."

The question was what we would do with it. Truthfully, I had no idea.

Trenton turned around in his chair. "And we're back."

It was so bizarre. I'd never expected to see any of the galaxy, and now I'd been to the other side. How did a girl from the Dark Planets reconcile all of this? It was going to take a minute for me to figure that out.

WE STEPPED ONTO MARS STATION, and I winced. I really hated this place. The fake air, the artificial gravity, it really wasn't for me. I turned to Blaze. "Last time we came here, you said you were getting rid of me."

He leaned over and kissed my temple. "I'm sorry."

"That's okay. I had sex with you for the very first time. I think you're forgiven."

His laugh never ceased to surprise me. Blaze was such a serious person. To make him laugh was like some kind of gift.

"I hate this place. I think I'd hate any space station."

Devil shook his head. "Me too. I like planets. Which one do you want to move to?"

"You want me to just pick one? Like on a space map, go *one two three* and randomly stick my finger on one?" I squeezed Dev's hand. "I've been exactly four places. Here. And this is a no. My home, which I need to let go, I think. The hot planet where we got taken and that was too rainy, too hot. And The Farm. Out of all of them, I like The Farm. Unless you'd like to go elsewhere."

Anders shrugged. "I like The Farm. But can we live some place off base? Like Waverly did but really, really farther. Like practically the other side of the planet?"

I understood what he was saying. It was important we have a lot of space. The eight of us weren't going to be normal, not ever, and we did better when left just to ourselves. Others could have crowds, we only needed each other.

Like we were our own group, made only to socialize among ourselves.

"Yes."

Anders liked that. His smile grew. "Great. I'll build us some place fantastic to live."

Kellan came up behind me. "Melissa is on her way here. She has people with her. And she's walking really, really fast."

I turned to look, and Wade rushed out in front of us. "What the hell?"

What was I missing? "Wade?"

Trenton shook his head. "That is his brother and sister."

The ones that were supposed to be in school?

Mars Station was crowded, but I watched as two people who shared Wade's distinct eye color and general look rushed toward him. They gripped onto his body, hugging him like their world might end if they didn't. He hugged them back, and my breath caught in my throat. What was happening here?

"They arrived yesterday, stowing on a ship. They heard Wade was here. Long ago rumor of some kind, and they wanted to see him. I was about to send them back to school, but here you are... so they can be your problem." Melissa pulled me into a hug.

It was awkward. I was never going to be great about hugging strangers. There was always that instinct that they were going to take from me, want to give me emotions I didn't want to own. But Melissa seemed to just want to hug, and so after I jerked against her, I let myself give the older woman a hug.

She'd traveled the galaxy so long ago and made a life for her family. I didn't have the slightest idea how we were going to do the same, but she was an example of success.

"I'm glad they're okay."

She waved her hand. "Good luck with them. I don't think those two are going to let themselves be sent off again. They really missed him. And teenagers are just toddlers with bigger vocabularies. So good luck handling that."

I snorted and then stopped. Oh wow, she wasn't kidding. No, I didn't have the slightest idea what to do with teenagers.

Wade walked over to us, his brother and sister under each of his arms. "This is Sienna. She's mine. Well, all of ours."

I stared at their faces with their wounded eyes and lost souls. I was familiar with those kinds of people. Yes, they'd fit in perfectly well with us. "It's so nice to have you two with us, finally. We have to figure out home. Can you help us with that?"

* * *

I let Dane and Wade run exactly two days' worth of tests on me before I'd had enough, and no one argued. We had to make our way to The Farm to start whatever life we were going to have. It didn't bother me that we didn't have a plan.

We had each other. That was enough of a plan. Sure, we'd have to make a living. Blaze was already talking to Nolan about opening some kind of academy where he would help train security they could put out over the galaxy to protect the autonomy of various planets.

I didn't know if that would work, but I doubted I'd play a role in it. When Canyon had spoken to me from the future, he'd said something about our kids being friends. That idea suited me just fine. I'd never thought I could have a family. If that were a possibility, I'd be glad to get started on that.

Besides, it looked like I was going to be playing makeshift big sister-slash-mother to two teenagers who seemed to alternate between elation and anger pretty rapidly just in a matter of days.

As we pulled away from Mars Station, leaving Melissa Alexander and all that was hers where they ruled, I stood in the center of seven men who loved me. This was a ferry to The Farm. None of us had to fly this ship.

We were leaving the one who had taken us and so many like us on the journeys of our lifetimes behind where she would finally be retired. She was ending, but I was starting. I didn't know exactly where the arrow I'd pointed would land.

For now, there were no signs of Evander. Perhaps I'd accidently saved the universe.

I didn't know.

But I was looking forward to finding out.

* * *

Artemis

. . .

It was quiet, and I was glad for the lack of noise. Not that I'd minded, all of those years. It wasn't clear when I'd become aware of them all. It was like one day they were all there. The girl who had taken me and then lost her memory but found a new life inside of my walls. Then her daughter got lost and found until she knew herself. When had that little girl become a woman? How had that happened so fast? She had a best friend who drove herself mad trying to be enough until she realized she was more than that already. Her sister-in-law saved everyone but never stopped doubting herself until her loves let her feel okay for the first time. Then the beautiful doctor who had to dig deep for her strength but then became a force of nature.

And finally the lost girl. The last one. She hadn't quite fit in until she discovered that all you needed for happiness was your own people to understand you, and then the rest of the universe didn't matter.

There had been so many explosions. So much commotion. I was glad to take all of it.

But now it was time to sleep.

The first girl was back. She walked into where they were going to let me rest. This was her place, her station. I could feel her everywhere here. She placed her hand on my hull.

"Thank you."

She was more than welcome. They all were.

Goodnight.

Dear Reader,

Thank you so much for having taken this ride with me. I will miss these characters and still can't believe it is done!

You might be thinking about trying something else from me? Please turn the page and see the long list of 106 books I've published, most of them completed series.

All of my thanks,
    Rebecca Royce

As a teenager, I would hide in my room to read my favorite romance novels when I was supposed to be doing my homework.

I am the mother of three adorable boys and I am fortunate to be married to my best friend. I live in Austin Texas where I am determined to eat all the barbecue in town.

I am in love with science fiction, fantasy, and the paranormal and try to use all of these elements in my writing. I've been told I'm a little bloodthirsty so I hope that when you read my work you'll enjoy the action packed ride that always ends in romance. I love to write series because I love to see characters develop over time and it always makes me happy to see my favorite characters make guest appearances in other books.

In my world anything is possible, anything can happen, and you should suspect that it will.

I'd love to hear from you! Please visit my website at www.rebeccaroyce.com to sign up for my newsletter and learn about my books!

Here's where you can find me online:

Rebecca's Randomness Reading Group https://www.facebook.com/groups/RebeccasRandomness/

https://www.rebeccaroyce.com

https://www.facebook.com/authorrebeccaroyce/

www.twitter.com/rebeccaroyce

Instagram: rebeccaroyce79
Cheers!!
Rebecca

Redheads

Redhead on the Run https://amzn.to/2Nb3RcH

Redheaded Redemption (Coming Soon)

Wings of Artemis (completed series)

Kidnapped By Her Husbands https://amzn.to/2BQdUxy

Rescued by Their Wife https://amzn.to/2Rr9as4

Crashing Into Destiny https://amzn.to/2VkyXRL

Meeting Them https://amzn.to/2BLPaXm

Reclaiming Their Love https://amzn.to/2GKAw8E

Loving Them https://amzn.to/2BKDmEK

Ship Called Malice https://amzn.to/2BNputj

Saving Them https://amzn.to/2SsrBtH

Dark Demise https://amzn.to/2VidXv3

Light Unfolding https://amzn.to/2GO6Yqr

Still Waters https://amzn.to/2CFePT8

Rising Tides https://amzn.to/2MCdTlM

Lost Star https://amzn.to/2X8hcZA

Pointed Arrow https://amzn.to/3gK9tYH

Last Hope (completed series)

Tradition Be Damned

Past Be Damned

Destiny Be Damned

Compassion Be Damned

Future Be Damned

Dragon Wars (completed series)

Forever

Eternal

Always

Evermore

Endless

Wards and Wands (completed series)

Hexed and Vexed

Curse Reversed

Meow, Baby (novella, co-written with Ripley Proserpina)

Tragic Magic

Safe Haven

Everywhere and Nowhere

Dimension X (coming soon)

More coming soon....

Soul Bound

Prisoner of the Dragons

More coming soon....

Shadow Promised

Strange Days

Weird Nights

Bizarre Years

More coming soon...

The Warrior (completed series)

Initiation

Driven

Subversive

Redemption

Justice

Warrior World (spin off of The Warrior, completed series)

Deacon

Micah

Jason

The Westervelt Wolves (completed series)

Her Wolf

Summer's Wolf

Wolf Reborn

Wolf's Valentine

Wolf's Magic

Alpha Wolf

Angel's Wolf

Darkest Wolf

Lone Wolf

Fallen Alpha

Alpha Rising

Alpha's Strength

Alpha's Sacrifice

Alpha's Truth

Alpha Enticing

Hidden Alpha (coming soon)

Illicit Minds

Illicit Senses

Illicit Connections

Illicit Alliance (coming soon)

The Outsiders

Love Beyond Time

Love Beyond Sanity

Love Beyond Loyalty

Love Beyond Sight

Love Beyond Expectations

Love Beyond Oceans

Love Beyond Flames

Love Beyond Lies

Love Beyond Death (coming soon)

Cascade (completed series)

Haunted Redemption

Phoenix Everlasting

Fragility Unearthed

Persuasion Enraptured

Reverse Harem Story (completed series)

Unconventional

Unexpected

Undeniable

Kiss Her Goodbye (completed series)

Hard Truths

Dark Truths

Deadly Truths

Shifter World

Planet Bear

Planet Wolf (coming soon)

The Swamp

Hidden

Pursued

Caught

Stand Alone Titles

Under The Lights

No Quitting Allowed

Mr. Wrong

Bite Marks

Bitten Surrender

The Vampire and The Virgin

Demon Within

Crimson Lust

Call Me Crazy

The Men of Elite Metal

The Storm (writing with Ripley Proserpina) **completed series.**

Lightning Strikes

Thunder Rolling

The Deluge

Heart of the Nebula (writing with Heather Long) **completed series**

Queenmaker

Deal Breaker

Throne Taker

Stupid Boys (writing with C.R. Jane)

Stupid Boys

Dumb Girl

Crazy Love

Through the Gates (writing with Skye MacKinnon)

Purgatory City

Infernal Land

The Coveted (writing with Ripley Proserpina)

Eyes in the Darkness

Voices in the Darkness

Return to the Darkness

Prison Princess (part of the Prison Princess world, writing with CoraLee June)

www.ingramcontent.com/pod-product-compliance
Lightning Source LLC
Chambersburg PA
CBHW011508170626
46812CB00009B/3015